Chapter One

The ugliest case which Carolus Deene ever chose to
investigate was brought to his notice by his housekeeper Mrs Stick, a little woman whose aim had
always been to keep Carolus away from 'murders and
such'. Perhaps she was not conscious of what she
would be starting when she said primly one Sunday
evening—'Stick's very upset.' Carolus, who was accustomed to hearing somewhat enigmatic references to
his housekeeper's husband, obligingly asked—'What
about?'

'You'd better ask him,' said Mrs Stick. 'I can't get a
word out of him. It's something he's seen on the Boxley
Road. He won't say what it is, but I daresay he'll tell
you, being a man. All I know is, it's put him off his
supper tonight and that means it's not to be laughed
at. When Stick's off his food he *has* been upset and
no mistake about it.'

'I'll ask him about it in the morning,' promised
Carolus, who was preparing to turn in.

But ten minutes later Mrs Stick returned to his
study, her face flushed and her whole small being
showing excitement which she could not repress.

'I've got it out of him,' she said. 'You can't wonder
he didn't want to say anything about it. It's scarcely
decent, not for a lady to hear.'

Carolus knew better than to interrupt.

'Stick was walking back from the Three Thistles at Boxley this evening when a car came up behind him and almost knocked him into the hedge. I've told him a hundred times to walk facing the traffic if he must walk at all along the road at night, but he won't listen. The car didn't stop, of course, and there was Stick pushed right in the ditch or culvert or whatever they call it. He was just going to climb back on to the road when he saw this arm ...'

'Which arm?'

'What I'm telling you about. It was an arm stretched out there, and when Stick stooped down and looked he saw the whole body lying in the ditch. But what upset him was that this fellow hadn't a stitch on. Can you imagine it?'

'Not until you tell me which fellow.'

'How do I know which fellow? Stick says he looked about seventeen but you couldn't really tell because he was stone dead. Been some time, Stick said, and his face covered with bruises.'

'Did Stick recognize him?'

'No. Well, he wouldn't, would he? I mean it might have been anyone. Might not have come from round here at all.'

'What did Stick do?'

'Do? What could he do? He looked round for something to cover the poor young fellow up. At least to make him a bit decent for anyone who came on him, like Stick had. All he could find was the *News of the People* which he had in the pocket of his overcoat meaning to have a read of it when he got home. So he put that over and came back here as fast as he could.'

'He has not reported what he found?'

'He was going to tell you as soon as he got his breath, you being interested in anything like that.'

'Like what, Mrs Stick?'

'Well, murders and that. I mean, what else could it be?'

'An accident,' suggested Carolus not very convincingly.

'What, with no clothes on?'

'They could have been removed after death.'

'I suppose they could have but it doesn't seem likely, does it?'

'Suicide?'

'I suppose it might be that, but who's going to kill himself with nothing on unless he was raving mad? No, Stick thinks he'd been murdered. That's why he was going to tell you about it.'

'It will have to be reported,' said Carolus. 'Will you ask Stick if he'll drive out with me and show me where it is?'

'That's what he said he wanted to do. You know what Stick is. He'd rather you took charge of it than go running round to the police station and have them asking all sorts of questions.'

'Very well. I'll get the car out,' said Carolus rising.

'He'll wait for you out by the gate,' promised Mrs Stick.

Little was said as Carolus drove out in the direction of Boxley for Stick was a man of few words. He did say 'I couldn't believe my eyes when I saw what it was,' but after that he kept silence till he told Carolus that 'it must be about here' and Carolus pulled up.

'It' was just there. Almost exactly where Stick had asked Carolus to stop. By the light of his powerful torch Carolus examined the body when Stick had removed the copy of the *News of the People* with which he had covered it 'to make the poor young fellow a bit decent' as Mrs Stick had explained.

The boy—Carolus judged him to be even younger than seventeen—lay in a peculiar hunched-up position. *Rigor mortis*, that stiffness so popular with crime writers, had produced a weird effect as though down there in the ditch he was sitting hunched on the pillion of an invisible motor-bike, his arms stretched out as though they had been clasped round the rider's waist. But as Mrs Stick had put it in a prim cliché he had 'not a stitch on'. What was more there were patches and swellings on his face.

Carolus noticed another thing. Round each wrist was a ring of abrasions in the flesh as though he had been handcuffed or tied with rope. Since the two rings were similar, identical in fact, it would seem that the dead boy had been roped by the wrists. Almost instinctively Carolus looked down at the ankles and found similar rings of red rubbed flesh.

'Looks as though he's had his hair cut,' remarked Stick and Carolus, having followed Stick's pointing finger agreed. But the job had not been done by a skilled barber. The dead boy had worn his hair long and probably since his death it had been roughly shorn.

Stick excelled himself. 'Must have been done after he was dead,' he said. 'Those that have long hair don't like parting with it. It's taken a long time to grow, you see, and they're proud of it. So I should say if I were asked...' He looked at Carolus as though he wanted encouragement ... 'that it had been done after he was dead and knew nothing about it.'

Carolus did not answer. He was looking down on the dead boy and his face was serious, even sad. Whatever the youngster was, whatever he had done to be killed, he was a pitiful sight. He was at the very beginning of those years which are the best in most lives. And in the light of the torch his face had not the placid, sometimes rather beautiful expression of dead youth. He looked as though he had died in agony.

Perhaps Stick thought the same.

'I'd like to know what killed him,' he remarked to Carolus.

'So would I. And who. But we can leave that to the police. I've seen all I want to here. You'd better stay here to see that no one touches him while I drive back to the police station. It won't take me more than a quarter of an hour and the police will soon be out. You don't mind, Stick?'

'I can't say I fancy it and the wife will get jumpy if I don't get home soon. But I see what you mean. We don't want anyone messing about with the evidence, do we? So you run along, sir, and I'll wait here.'

Carolus drove away. It was only a few months since he had admitted that his attempt to retire from his mastership at the Queen's School, Newminster, had been a failure and he had returned to the small Georgian house in the town which he had let on a short lease, foreseeing perhaps that he would need it again. He had, moreover, returned to the School on a part-time basis, giving history lessons to the senior students, but not as a full member of the staff. This had suited him admirably and the scheme had been welcomed by the Headmaster, Mr Gorringer, particularly as Carolus, who had large private means, asked that his salary should be paid to the school's Re-Building Fund.

The Sticks were delighted to be back in the house

in which they had looked after Carolus for nearly thirty years and all that had been wanting in Carolus's life had been one of those deathly puzzles, which more frivolous observers called whodunnits, to occupy his time and test his powers of deduction. And this Sunday evening it looked as though the need had been filled. He was, as he might have thought, At It Again and all set. At least he had been presented with a corpse. The rest, in his experience, would shortly follow.

He entered Newminster Police Station, regretting the days when John Moore had been the senior CID man in the place and they had worked together so successfully. John was now Detective Superintendent Moore of the Yard and there was a strange face behind the uniformed duty sergeant's desk.

'Sergeant Patson, I believe,' said Carolus who had troubled to become informed about the Newminster Police.

'That's right. What can I do for you?' said the sergeant curtly.

'I've come to report a dead body.'

'Have you now? Would your name be Deene by any chance? Yes? I've heard about you, Mr Deene. Is this one of your practical jokes?'

'No. Nor any other kind of a joke. A boy of about sixteen is lying in the ditch beside the Boxley Road, naked and dead.'

Sergeant Patson no longer smiled.

'I'm sorry,' he said. 'You have a bit of a reputation for pulling our legs. I thought you were doing it this time.' He pulled a writing pad towards him. 'Did you find the body yourself?'

'No. My gardener did. He was walking home from Boxley when a car nearly pushed him in the ditch and drove on. In the ditch was the dead boy.'

Patson was evidently quite serious when he asked, 'Did he notice the number of the car?'

Carolus kept his temper.

'No. He did not notice the number of the car. But he noticed that he had nearly fallen on top of a dead youth who was stiff and huddled up. And he reported it to me.'

'Why didn't he come to the police?' asked Sergeant Patson.

'My house was nearer. I told him to get in my car and guide me to the place.'

'That was very unwise of you, Mr Deene. A discovery of this sort should be reported immediately to the police, not to a private individual, however much he may fancy himself as an investigator. Where did you say the cadaver is to be found?'

'I didn't say. And if you talk like the *Police Manual* I shan't say. So let's stop all this high horse nonsense and I'll speak to your CID officer, if he's in.'

Sergeant Patson gave Carolus a nasty look. A very nasty look. But he picked up his telephone and spoke to someone whom he addressed as 'Harold'.

'Detective Sergeant Grimsby will be here in a few minutes,' he said sulkily.

'I'll wait for ten,' said Carolus and there was silence between them.

When Grimsby came in, wearing grey flannels and smoking a pipe, Patson nodded towards Carolus but did not find it necessary to say more.

'Yes, Mr Deene?' said Grimsby.

Noting that Grimsby too was aware of his name, Carolus said—'A youth is lying dead in a ditch by the Boxley Road.'

'Accident?'

'I shouldn't think so. He's stark naked. I'll drive you out there if you like.'

'I'll follow in my car, if you don't mind. May have to go off somewhere else. Shall we go?'

Carolus led the way and Grimsby kept close behind. Stick was waiting where Carolus had left him and Carolus explained his presence to Grimsby.

Grimsby made a brief businesslike examination then went to the telephone in his car. When he had set in motion what he called 'all the formalities' Carolus asked him to take statements from himself and Stick so that they could leave for home before all the police palaver began. Grimsby agreed to this.

'May have to ask you both to give us further details tomorrow,' he warned. 'But for this evening I can soon get down your statements.'

He proceeded to do so in a smart, almost military fashion. It did not seem that he gave the whole thing any great importance. One would have thought he was accustomed to finding dead young men in a ditch naked every day of the week. There was something rather callous about his handling of the dead limbs, too. Altogether a very unsentimental police officer, Carolus thought.

'Any idea how long he's been there?' asked Carolus.

'The doctor will tell us. I should guess about twenty-four hours,' Grimsby said. 'But it's only a guess.'

'No idea who he is, I suppose?' persisted Carolus.

'Never seen him before, but they all look alike nowadays. No need for you to hang about if you don't want to. Nor you Mr Stick.'

'Good. Then we'll go,' said Carolus. 'You know where I live if you want me again?'

'Yes. I know,' said Grimsby. 'Good night, Mr Deene.'

Mrs Stick was still up when they reached home.

'I suppose this will start you off again, sir,' she said rather sulkily. 'If I'd have known what it was Stick had found I shouldn't have said anything about it. Now I suppose we shall have nothing but murders for the next few weeks.'

'Only one,' Carolus corrected. 'If it *was* a murder. The police will know that.'

'So you're leaving it to the police? That's something, anyhow. I shan't have my heart in my mouth twenty times a day wondering who's at the front door. I only hope you mean what you say. It wouldn't be the first time you'd have got mixed up in something after you'd said you'd leave it to the police.'

'It depends on what they do about it,' said Carolus.

'There you go!' said Mrs Stick. 'I knew what it would be as soon as we got back to Newminster. I told Stick, I said, it won't be long before he gets started again on something horrible, I said. But I never thought when Stick came in looking upset it would lead to all this. The young fellow was dead, I suppose?'

'Quite, quite dead, Mrs Stick.'

'There you are. One of these long haired ones, sure to be?'

'No. His hair was short.'

'They're worse! A skinhead, you mean?'

'Not exactly. I think he'd had long hair but it had been cut off.'

'There! It makes you think, doesn't it? I suppose you'll find out all about who did that, won't you? I wonder you don't get tired of it all, I really do. Murder, murder, murder. Anyone would think you had nothing better to do. And Stick's as bad, putting you up to it. I don't know what Mr Gorringer will say when he knows. No sooner do we get back here and settle down when you're off looking for clues.

How did you say they'd killed the poor young fellow?'

'I didn't. I don't know. Good night, Mrs Stick. Sleep well.'

The little woman gave Carolus her fiercest stare as he left the room.

Chapter Two

When Grimsby came to see him a few days later, Carolus realized that it was not so much to obtain the necessary details about finding the body of the dead youth as to consult him as an expert. Not that he said so. A policeman would rather die than admit that he had anything to learn from an amateur dabbler in crime investigation, and in many ways he would be justified in holding Carolus, and his whole tribe, in contempt.

Professionalism in this as in most other ways of life was really to be admired and respected. The gifted amateur sometimes struck lucky but was usually to be dismissed as a nuisance.

But Grimsby was young and, as he admitted to Carolus, had been put in charge of the investigation in this case, given for the first time the responsibility of clearing up what his superiors had called a 'nasty mess'. He knew the reputation of Carolus and although he would not admit it had a half-mocking hope that Carolus would lean back in his chair, put his fingers together and proceed to solve the entire puzzle.

That there was a puzzle, and that he was baffled by it, Grimsby admitted to himself, adding in his own mind that there could be no harm in hearing what that chap Deene had to say. Carolus, on his side, knew that only through Grimsby could he learn the essential facts of the case, the identity of the murdered boy and perhaps something of his associates.

'Oh yes, we know who he was all right,' said Grimsby. 'There'll be no secret about it by tomorrow because we've given the name to the papers. The London Press aren't interested and even our local newspapers don't show much excitement. There's been so much of this sort of thing lately, you see. The novelty has worn off.'

'But the puzzles remain?'

'That's it. They do.'

Carolus was silent for a moment then said, 'Did you notice the dead boy's wrists?'

Grimsby looked disappointed. If this was all the famous Carolus Deene had to contribute it would not get him much farther.

'Yes. And his ankles,' he said. 'Been carried some distance on the pillion seat of a motor-cycle.'

'Dead or alive?'

'Either, as I see it. Probably dead. The boy came from Hartington. Father's a foreman in a plastics factory.'

'So you think the boy was murdered, stripped, and dumped in that ditch?'

'Or vice versa. No idea yet. The doctor says he'd been dead for at least twenty-four hours when you found him. He could have been killed in Hartington on the Saturday afternoon, in fact, and brought across to Newminster, (that's about thirty miles as you know) during the darkness of Saturday night.'

'His ankles tied to the footrests of a motor-cycle and his arms round the rider's waist. Wearing a helmet and goggles, perhaps?'

'Yes. Obviously.'

'But dead?'

'Could be.'

'Why was he stripped then?'

'Identification, I suppose. Or at least to delay identification. Actually, we knew on the third day that a Hartington youth known as "Dutch" Carver had been missing since Saturday afternoon. So the delay wasn't of much use, was it?'

'Not unless those two days were important to someone. They could have been.'

Grimsby considered that.

'Yes. I suppose so. The boy was a greaser. Had hair down to his shoulder blades. That, as you know, had been roughly cut.'

'I saw that.'

'And that's about as far as I've got. Obvious suspects are the skinheads of the town, particularly one group. Doesn't it seem a bit fantastic to you in this day and age that our murder suspects are quite often teenagers? It sickens me.'

'Yes. How many of the group are there?'

'About a dozen. I've questioned four without much satisfaction. You understand of course, that this conversation is in the strictest confidence, don't you?'

'Of course. I appreciate that. I'll tell you what I'm considering. The facts begin to interest me and I think I'll run over to Hartington. I don't like the place, but it's there that the core of this case would seem to lie. You needn't be aware I've gone or show that you know me if we meet. I shall work on my own and if I get anything for you I'll phone you here in Newminster.'

'Fine. I'll expect to hear from you.'

'Don't be too optimistic. I'm a bit out of my depths with all these young skinheads, greasers, hippies and muggers. But I shan't keep anything from you. Facts, I mean. Theories are my own affair till they are strong enough to hand over. Agreed?'

'Agreed. I'd like to see the D.S's face if he heard us exchanging those words. He's a sort of a caricature of a television Super. Has it ever occurred to you that Z Cars and the rest have materially influenced the Police Force? Life following Art, if you call them art.'

'Television policemen are infallible, invariably infallible,' said Carolus.

Grimsby did not rise to that. He pulled out a notebook and began to give Carolus some more detailed and factual information about Hartington and its people. This Carolus noted carefully. Then, after Grimsby had refused a drink, the policeman prepared to leave.

'I've purposely not given you any theories I may have, or am beginning to form,' said Grimsby. 'Because they're not worth having yet. You'll know more in an hour than I've been able to conclude in two days. I'm hoping you'll go your own way. But you won't be bored, Mr Deene. I can assure you of that.'

'My name's Carolus. And I'm not easily bored, especially by murder. It *was* murder, I suppose?'

'Yes. The boy had been suffocated after being tied up.'

'I rather thought that was how it was done. Poor little sod.'

'Don't be too ready with your sympathy till you've learned a bit more about him, Carolus.'

'I'll repress my kindly instincts.'

'Until you know there is cause for them.'

Grimsby smiled and left Carolus. His car was started and Carolus looked after its disappearing number plate.

Mrs Stick came in almost at once.

'I could see he was from the police,' she boasted. 'You can always tell. I suppose he'd come about the murder?'

'He wanted some details about the finding of the body.'

'I hope you told him what a nasty shock it was. Stick hasn't really got over it yet.'

She was stopped by a prolonged ringing of the front door bell. Her hand went to her heart with a rather exaggerated gesture.

'Whoever can that be?' she asked Carolus rhetorically as she went to the window. 'Oh. Thank goodness. It's only Mr Hollingbourne,' she added, naming one of Carolus's colleagues on the staff of the Queen's School, Newminster, a philoprogenitive character whose children already numbered seven. 'He won't have come about anything to do with murders, that's one sure thing.'

But Mrs Stick was wrong, for once. Hollingbourne, tall, humourless and usually somewhat hostile to Carolus whom he regarded as a playboy, sat bolt upright in a chair and announced unnecessarily—'I wanted to see you, Deene.'

Carolus nodded. There was nothing else to do.

'The Head tells me you are making enquiries about the young fellow found dead on Sunday night?'

Carolus, who disliked Hollingbourne's way of referring to Mr Gorringer as though he were an earthly deity, like a newspaper proprietor, again nodded.

'I can tell you something about him,' Hollingbourne said astoundingly.

'You can? How on earth does that happen?'

Hollingbourne got down to serious narrative.

'As you may know,' he said. 'The wife and I are

accustomed to take the children for a summer holiday
to the seaside. We choose some place with a sandy
beach where they can play cricket and so on. Those
that are old enough, that is.'

'Quite.'

'Three years ago it was to Kingsgate. Excellent
sands and not too far away.'

'Of course.'

'But unlike you, Deene, I was not provided by my
parents with a large private income and in order to
meet the expenses of a summer holiday for us all, I am
forced to seek some form of additional remuneration.'

'Coaching?' suggested Carolus.

'Not necessarily coaching, but adding to our numbers one or two young paying guests whose parents
want to give them a healthy seaside holiday.'

'Good heavens!' Carolus could not repress the ex-
clamation.

'We have discovered that catering for increased
numbers is comparatively economical. In a word, it
pays.'

'I see.'

'At first we agreed to limit the scheme to boys at
the school whose parents found it inconvenient to keep
them during the summer holidays. But lately we have
found that parents from what the Head calls more
plebeian backgrounds are those most able to afford to
take advantage of the scheme. In the year we went to
Kingsgate we had as a paying guest the son of a foreman in the All-Purpose Plastics Works at Hartington.
His name was Carver.'

'You're not going to tell me that it was the boy
whom Stick found dead on the Boxley Road?'

'Unless I am very much mistaken...' Hollingbourne's
tone made clear the near impossibility of this. 'It was

the same youth. In that case I advise you to have
nothing to do with his death.'

'But why not? It seems quite an interesting case.'

'Interesting? Interesting? The boy was a dangerous
schizophrenic. He induced my children to enter a cave
in the cliffside and lit a fire in the entrance to im-
prison them there.'

'All of them?' Carolus asked.

'Except the two smallest mites. They were fortunately with their mother. Had it not been for another
family who heard my children screaming I shudder to
think what might have happened. But that's not all.
He discovered a wardrobe dealer's shop in Kingsgate
and having pilfered the best part of the family wardrobe he sold it and spent the proceeds on going to
the cinema at times when I usually organized games on
the beach for us all.'

'I used to do that,' commented Carolus.

'He was rebellious and rude to my wife and even
took advantage of my own holiday spirit to steal the
light cigars I sometimes allow myself.'

'Whiffs?'

'That is their trade name. He was, in fact, a
thoroughly unsatisfactory boy from start to finish of
the holidays.'

'Oh. He stayed with you to the finish?'

'No,' said Hollingbourne gravely. 'He ran away.
That is partly why I thought you should know something of the young wretch. He ran away during the
night, or rather in the very early morning, and I had
to report it to the police. Most disagreeable. We had
never had any trouble of this kind before. They found
him...' Hollingbourne paused before bringing out his
punch line ... 'They found him in London. In the
West End. He was living on his...' another pause

which Carolus would like to have filled, then a con-
cluding 'wits', from Hollingbourne.

'How old was he then?'

'Under fourteen years. A born delinquent. It horri-
fies me to think that he associated with my children.
I feared for a long time that his influence might have
proved corrupting. One of the girls, the wife told me
at the time, used language that she can only have
learned from him.'

'What did she say?'

'It wasn't so much the words she used. Children
often use unpleasant words without understanding
them. It was her whole manner towards her mother
and me. Fortunately shortly afterwards she became a
tennis enthusiast, playing in several competitions, and
this seems to have given her a healthier interest. But
you see the dangers when a young scoundrel of that
sort enters a decent household?'

'You haven't seen him since, of course?'

'Certainly not. I told his father to keep him away,
explaining the anxiety he had caused us.'

'What did his father say?' asked Carolus curiously.

'His remarks were unprintable. One saw at once
where the influence came from, though I did not gather
there was any love lost between father and son. One
of his choicer threats was to "wring the little bleeder's
throat". But I'm glad to say that from that summer
onwards I have seen nothing of the family and only
when the Head told me that you were interested in the
boy's death...'

'He told you that? I wonder how he got hold of it.'

'News travels fast in Newminster,' said Hollingbourne. 'You can't hush things up. By the way, have
you heard that Tubley's getting married again?'

'Tubley?' repeated Carolus incredulously. Tubley

was another colleague, the music master on the staff.
'Who is...'

'Another link with Hartington. She teaches at the
Technical School there.'

'Really? Then I shall probably meet her. I'm going
to be in Hartington for the next week or two.'

'I thought you might be, in spite of my warning.
Snooping, I suppose? I doubt if the Head will approve
of that but of course,' conceded Hollingbourne, 'it's
none of my business. I simply came to give you an
idea about the young brute whose death you find it
necessary to investigate.'

'Not necessary. Interesting,' said Carolus. 'Which is
where we came in.'

Mrs Stick returning said—'You haven't offered Mr
Hollingbourne a drink, sir.'

'I've been so interested in what he has been telling
me,' said Carolus apologetically, 'that I quite forgot my
manners. Hollingbourne?'

'A glass of sherry,' said Hollingbourne cheerfully.
'If you have a rather sweet one.'

Carolus made a grimace.

'I expect so. Mrs Stick?'

'There's the Amoroso,' said Mrs Stick doubtfully.

'That will do,' said Hollingbourne. 'You have a
strange hobby, Deene. It would not do for me. So
much else to do.'

'I daresay you have. Your wife quite well?'

'Splendid, thanks. She's taking our oldest up to the
oculist's today. We believe in looking after their eyes.
Here's to your very good health.'

Carolus responded suitably and soon afterwards
Hollingbourne left.

'I thought when I saw him coming to the door,' Mrs

Stick said, looking somewhat secretive, 'that it was his wife again.'

'But he wouldn't come here for that,' said Carolus anxiously

'You never know. They haven't got a telephone,' said Mrs Stick.

'I'm going to Hartington this afternoon,' Carolus told her. 'May stay over there for a few days. I'll let you know where I'm staying if I do.'

'I shan't say anything,' replied Mrs Stick ambiguously. 'It's no good, is it? I'll just have to expect you when I see you. What shall I tell anyone who asks for you?'

'No one will. Unless it happens to be Mr Gorringer.'

'Well what shall I tell him? He's bound to be round as soon as he hears that you've gone.'

'Tell him that I've gone away for a few days. To see a man about a murder,' Carolus added, and left Mrs Stick looking after him with evident disapproval.

Chapter Three

Among the pieces of information which Grimsby had given Carolus were some details about the dead boy's father.

'You'll find Herbert Carver at 21 Crapper Place,' he said. 'Named after a former Mayor. Unfortunate as a street-name, isn't it? Carver is living with a butcher's wife, Mrs Farnham.'

'What about the boy's mother?'

'Oh she's living with a West Indian, Justus Delafont.'

'I see. Then how about the butcher? I suppose he's living with the West Indian's wife?'

'No. He's queer,' said Grimsby shortly.

So as he drove through the outlying streets of Hartington, consisting of crowded little houses with mini lawns in front of them, Carolus pondered on these marital, and extra-marital complications. Then as it was early in the evening, the time at which a foreman in a plastics factory might be expected to be home, he decided to call on Herbert Carver, the boy's legitimate father.

The bell was answered by a bad-tempered looking woman in a chintz overall.

'Yes. He's in,' she said sharply to Carolus's enquiry.

'I'll see if he's finished his tea. Wait a minute.'

She was not long absent and said, 'You can come in if you want, only you'll have to excuse me. I've got work to do.'

Carolus found Herbert Carver in a leatherette armchair. He was a solid-looking man in his late forties and smoked a pipe. He put aside an evening paper as Carolus entered.

'Come to ask about my boy?' he said. 'I thought so. I've had a lot of them here earlier, waiting as soon as I got in from work, and the police yesterday and the day before. What is it you want to know? He was no good. I can tell you that, same as I told all the others. Not like his brother.'

'I didn't know he had a brother,' Carolus said.

'Oh yes he had. Older than him. Lives with his mother. See, we separated. No other way for it. She was one of those always fancying herself being chased by someone. You know—romantic. One day I'd come home and she'd say it was the man next door was after her. Another day it was the postman. At the last I told her, if you think they're all chasing you, I said, you try being on your own and see how you get on. So that's what she did and all she's got is this black fellow.'

'You were saying that you had an older son?'

'That's right. The two of them. Roger and Kenneth, only the lads always called Kenneth "Dutch", I don't know why.'

'Kenneth stayed with you?'

'I suppose you could call it that. He was out most of the time. Mrs Farnham—that's my housekeeper as you might say—was always on about it. Out every night with a whole crowd of long-haired layabouts. I told her to let him get on with it. I wasn't going to interfere. If he wanted to hang round the Spook Club...'

'Is that a discotheque?' asked Carolus.

'Yes. Belongs to a fellow called Swindleton. They say he makes money out of it. I don't know how, because none of them that hang round there seem to have a ha'penny. But that's where that boy of mine used to spend his time. I scarcely ever saw him and, to tell you the honest truth, that didn't worry me, though he'd given up long ago asking me for money.'

'You didn't give him any?'

'You must be joking. Give him any? To spend on pot and lousy little teenage tarts? I'm not that stupid.'

'Was the discotheque you mentioned, the Spook Club, the only one in the town?'

'There's several of them. In a town like this where there's plenty of work for the teenagers if they want it, there's a lot of them got more money than they know what to do with. These discotheques are crowded at night just like the bingo halls for their mothers in the afternoons. People complain of the noise but they don't seem able to stop it. Perhaps they'll take some notice now, when one of the kids has been murdered.'

'Your kid, Mr Carver.'

'I suppose you're going to blame me for it? I tell you I scarcely saw anything of him.'

'There is a suggestion that one, or perhaps more, of the other youngsters was responsible.'

'So they may have been. The short-haired lot. Skinheads they call them. I don't know anything about that. One's as bad as the other as far as I'm concerned.'

A door at the back of the room, presumably leading to the kitchen, was suddenly opened and Mrs Farnham appeared. It was obvious that she had heard the men's conversation and wished to make no secret of it.

'No, and we don't want anything to do with them,' she said angrily. 'If Bert's son likes to get himself killed it's no business of ours. He shouldn't have gone about with a crowd like that, then perhaps he'd still be alive.'

'I told him so, long ago when he first started it,' said Carver.

'When was that?'

'Well, he's never been what you'd call a well-behaved boy. He's got into no end of trouble even when he was no more than nine or ten years old. It's like most of them nowadays, only he was worse. When he started doing things that the police took notice of, I left it to them. I'd got my job to think of and couldn't afford to go on paying fines for the property he damaged and that.'

'I should think not!' said Mrs Farnham. 'It was bad enough Roger going off with his mother and leaving Kenneth for us to look after. Roger's never given a bit of trouble and now he's started work at the factory it means he's a help instead of a hindrance like Kenneth's been. I told Bert from the first, I said he ought to have kept the older one of the two and let their mother take Kenneth, then we shouldn't have had all this trouble.'

'*Has* it meant so much trouble for you?' asked Carolus mildly.

'Of course it has, with the police round here and everything else. Then I suppose there'll be an inquest and goodness knows what. Anyone would think we'd murdered him the way they go on, instead of him very nearly murdering us when he set fire to the bed clothes, smoking half the night and half drugged for all I know. Pot, he called it, though the police told me it was cannabis. They used to get it from ...'

'We don't *know* that,' put in Bert Carver. 'It's only what you've been told. You want to be careful of saying things like that. We don't know where he got it from.'

'Still. You could tell by his eyes. He'd come down in the morning looking like I don't know what. It was all this cannabis they talk about.'

'Cannabis costs money,' Carolus said.

'Oh he always had plenty of money. You should see the clothes he had and the things he bought for himself. You know, radio sets and that. He must have a hundred or more records up in his room. Talk about money . . .'

'Where did he get it from, that's what I want to know,' said his father. 'It wasn't as though he ever did a stroke of work. I wouldn't put him past thieving if it came to that. It's like you read about with all these young fellows nowadays, they won't work but they expect to be given everything. Kenneth was just the same. I often wondered where he did get it from.'

'You never asked him?' tried Carolus.

'What would have been the good? It would only have meant more lies. I let him get on with it.'

'You don't think, perhaps, that your "letting him get on with it", as his father, I mean, may have caused some of the trouble?'

'Certainly not. I knew my own son, didn't I? I tried to use a bit of discipline when he was younger. But it was no good. I told him he was a proper little rotter, didn't I, Con?'

'All the same,' Carolus persisted. 'There must have been some good in your son.'

'I don't know where, then,' said Mrs Farnham. 'I could never see any good.'

'Dutch kept on with his singing,' said Bert Carver,

perhaps trying wearily to defend him.

'Singing? What singing? Oh, you mean with the Pop group. I don't see what good it did him. They can all do it, come to that. All they do is make a racket to keep you awake.'

'No. I meant in the choir.'

Carolus looked almost startled.

'The choir? You mean a church choir?'

'Yes, well, when he was a little youngster I used to send him down there with his brother to get him out of the way and stop him getting into mischief. Roger never took to it but young Kenneth fancied himself singing solos, with half the old women looking at him. They put him on to sing when the BBC did a television show of the church. That caused quite a lot of talk and Kenneth was running round like a dog with two tails.'

'I don't see that showed anything,' said Mrs Farnham. 'Just because he happened to have a good voice, that didn't make him an angel.'

'Still it must have meant some work and study,' Carolus pointed out.

'Must have done, *for the choirmaster*,' said Mrs Farnham contemptuously. 'I don't see Kenneth doing any study.'

'So you couldn't see any good in the boy at all?' Carolus asked Mrs Farnham, almost pleading this time.

'No. I couldn't,' she replied emphatically.

'He used to look after that little girl of Mrs Bodmin's, didn't he?' said Bert, who seemed to have come to his son's defence.

'The less said about that the better,' Mrs Farnham rejoined. 'She's only twelve now and they say...'

'You don't want to believe everything you hear,' interrupted Bert. 'I don't know where you get these things from, I really don't.' He turned to Carolus. 'If you want to hear something good about the boy, don't come to us, but go to Mrs Bodmin, the mother of the little girl I'm talking about. She'll tell you. And you might try his brother Roger.'

'What about his mother?'

'I should keep away from her, if I was you,' said Mrs Farnham. 'That is unless you want a knife in your back from that Jamaican or whatever he is. Besides, she'll say the same as what we do about Kenneth. She knows the truth, you see. Of course, you can *ask* her,' conceded Mrs Farnham. 'Only she's never had any time for Kenneth. She's got too much to do imagining things about herself. Wait till you see her. Then you won't wonder why...'

'All right. All right,' said Bert. 'That's enough of her. The only other person you're likely to hear anything good about Kenneth from is Mr Leng, the choirmaster. You can try Swindleton who keeps the discotheque but he's more likely to tell you how much pot Kenneth flogs for him.'

'Now who's making accusations?' asked Mrs Farnham. 'But I can tell you one thing. There isn't one of the young girls in the place has a good word to say for him.'

'But you say he has some friends?'

'Friends? Greasers like himself. They won't say anything, one way or the other. You can try, of course. You'll find them down at Swindleton's. The Spook Club it's called—I think I told you. It'll be a waste of time. You'd far better go to the Cattle Market...'

'Where's that?'

'That's what they call another discotheque, where the skinheads go. You might find out something there about Kenneth.'

'What good it'll do I *don't* know,' said Mrs Farnham. 'The boy's been killed and that's the end of it. I don't see what you want to go raking things up for.'

'I want to know who killed him,' said Carolus.

'Why? Why do you want to know that?' said Bert Carver in a frankly puzzled way.

Carolus considered. Why was he spending time on finding out who murdered a seemingly worthless youngster? There was no logical answer. The pursuit for the love of it. Art for Art's sake, he reflected. But he answered sharply—'I don't quite know. Perhaps I find myself siding with a boy whom everyone seems to condemn. Perhaps I was rather like that myself. At any rate I'm going to find out who killed him.'

'And send him away for a few years, I suppose,' said Bert.

'Him, *or her*,' Carolus responded.

'Don't look at me when you say that,' said Mrs Farnham. 'I scarcely knew the boy and what I did know I wouldn't have touched with a barge-pole.'

'I don't know where to look yet,' admitted Carolus. 'But I shall, Mrs Farnham. I can assure you that I shall.'

'You know what I say?' asked Bert. 'I say you get on with it. And all the rest of them that can't mind their own business. You get on with it, and the best of British Luck to you.'

'Thank you,' said Carolus. 'It looks as though I shall need it if the rest of the boy's friends and relatives are not more co-operative than you.'

'What should we co-operate about, I should like to know?' said Mrs Farnham. 'We've told you all we can.'

'Except anything which might possibly be of the smallest assistance to me.'

'We didn't even know he was missing till the Monday morning when we found he'd not been in all night.'

'But from your accounts there was nothing unusual about that?'

'Oh yes there was,' said Mrs Farnham. 'He didn't like missing his sleep. He'd come in after we'd gone to bed and not get up all day the next day until just before his father was coming home. Then he'd start dressing himself up and sneak away out before Bert could see him.'

'What about food?'

'He'd go to the Lucknow Restaurant some days, and some days to one of the cafés. But except sometimes on a Saturday he'd always come in at night. I used to hear him creeping upstairs when I was trying to get to sleep.'

'How did you know where he went to eat?'

'Roger told his dad that. I never saw him in the town myself. He was very deceitful. Never told anyone about himself. Even Roger didn't know much. That's why we can't tell the police all they want to know.'

'You go round and see that little girl's mother,' advised Bert Carver. 'She'll tell you more than what we can.'

'Yes. You go,' Mrs Farnham said challengingly. 'You'll find her at home now if you go straight away. 47 Docker Street, her address is. Her husband died a year or two back from a stroke while he was at work. One minute he was having a cup of tea and the next he was Gone, but his heart had been bad for some time the doctor said. She gets his pension of course and they've given her a job in the canteen where I used to work before I met my husband. I ought to have stayed there only how can you tell? This Farnham looked such a nice fellow. I never dreamt there was anything like that about him. You'll find Mrs Bodmin is all on her own, and always will be by the look of her. I said to Bert the other day, I said, she looks more like a skeleton than a human being. But I must say she works hard in that canteen.'

'What about the little girl?'

'She's at school all day. Her mother hasn't got the time to look after her. They say she has to do everything for herself, even mend her own clothes and make her bed. It's no life for a child of that age. Her mother ought to try and get married again, only where it is, she's . . .'

'That's enough,' said Bert. 'You're always on about someone. Let the man judge for himself.'

'Yes. Well, that's where you'll find her. 47 Docker Street. It's the house with the nasturtiums growing over the porch so you're bound to know it. She'll tell you about young Kenneth. More than you want to hear, very likely. If she doesn't know I don't know who does. They say she's given him all her husband's things . . .'

'Who says?' asked Bert angrily. 'Trust you to know better than anyone else. His sister took her husband's things home with her, what there was.'

'That's not what I heard,' said Mrs Farnham. 'Anyway, you pop round and try her. It's not ten minutes. Turn to the left at the corner and keep straight on by the Wheatsheaf. She'll be in now, sure to be. You'll very likely find the little girl as well if she hasn't gone to the pictures. She's a Caution! Liz her name is, her father having called her after the Queen. She's a little monkey but you can't help laughing. I shouldn't

tell her you've seen me. She might get the wrong idea.
You ask her about...'

'He'll ask her what he sees fit to ask her,' said Bert
and Carolus made for the door.

Chapter Four

At first it seemed that Carolus would not have a chance to ask Mrs Bodmin anything, for at 47 Docker Street the door was opened by a small girl who spoke in monosyllables and very unwillingly at that.

'Is Mum in?' Carolus asked, believing this was the most appropriate form of address for such an occasion.

The little girl shook her head.

'Will she be in soon, do you think?'

The little girl nodded.

'May I come in and wait for her?'

This caused the little girl to stare at him critically and long.

'Yes,' she said finally.

Carolus followed her into a sitting-room.

'You have a friend called Dutch, haven't you?'

Another nod.

'Have you seen him lately?'

'Mum says he's gone away.'

'I expect you're sorry?'

'He gave me a motor-car,' said the little girl unexpectedly.

'A toy one?'

'It goes fast. D'you want to see it?'

'Yes.'

Without another word the small girl began to climb the stairs. She brought down a toy car, to Carolus's inexpert eye it seemed an expensive one. Carolus did not know what prompted him to ask his next question.

'Has your Mum seen it?'

The small girl shook her head with some energy.

'Why not?'

'Dutch said not.'

As though reminded of that prohibition, the child took the toy upstairs again.

'Does Dutch often give you things?'

'Sweets. And sausage rolls. And fruit jellies. And coke. And coconut cakes. And a pencil for school...'

Carolus called a halt to this catalogue which promised to be interminable.

'Does your Mum give you things?'

'Sometimes but not like Dutch. Dutch gives me things I want.'

'Are they all secrets?'

'Yes. Dutch says not to tell.'

'What mustn't you tell?'

A rather vacant look came across the face. Carolus realized that the child's mind was somewhat retarded. Mental age about seven, he thought.

'Lots of things,' she said with a sly look.

'Aren't you going to tell me?'

Liz shook her head.

'Dutch won't give me any more presents if I tell.'

'Is there a secret between you and Dutch?'

The head shook slowly from side to side.

'Who is it about?'

'Shan't tell.'

'About your Mum?'

'No.'

There was the sound of a key in the lock followed by the entrance of a very pale gaunt woman who stared at Carolus with—hostility, was it? Or curiosity?

'Mrs Bodmin?' asked Carolus rising. 'I must apologize for coming in. Liz invited me. I wanted to see you.'

Before answering him Mrs Bodmin turned to her daughter.

'Run outside and play,' she said, 'while I talk to the gentleman. Run along, now, there's a good girl.'

Liz went.

'Sit down,' said Mrs Bodmin fairly amicably to Carolus. 'Are you from the Insurance Company?'

'No, Mrs Bodmin. I wanted to ask you about the boy they call Dutch Carver.'

Mrs Bodmin looked up as though she was startled. After a moment she said quietly, 'What about him?'

'I have been told I might hear something good about him if I asked you. Up till now everyone seems to have seen the worst side of his character.'

Mrs Bodmin looked at him narrowly.

'Have you been talking to Connie Farnham?'

'Yes. I went to see his father.'

'She's a bitch,' said Mrs Bodmin, with unexpected venom. 'A real bitch. She made that poor boy's life a misery as soon as she got hold of his father. I suppose she said he took drugs and that?'

'She suggested something of the sort.'

'She would. Just because she married a man that does nothing but run after boys, she has to turn his father against poor young Dutch.'

'I didn't get the impression that he needed much turning.'

'Well, he might not have, but she made it worse. Dutch wasn't a bad boy, Mr . . .'

'Deene,' said Carolus.

'He wasn't a bad boy, Mr Deene. Only he'd never had anyone to look after him. His mother going off with that African fellow ...'

'I heard he was a Jamaican.'

'Whatever he was. And his father picking up with that Connie Farnham after her husband had left her, you can't wonder at young Ken's being a bit of a black sheep, can you? But there was no real harm in him. Ever so generous he was, too. He was always giving my little Liz presents.'

'She seems to have been quite attached to him.'

'She was. Of course I hadn't the time to look after her all day, but I often said he was as good as a mother with her.'

'You never felt the least concern about her when she was with Kenneth Carver?'

'With Dutch? No, none at all.'

'You don't think there was anything she didn't tell you? Any sort of secret between them?'

'If you're getting at what I think you are you can put that out of your head at once. Ken used to sing in the choir, you know.'

'You think that's a guarantee of virtue, Mrs Bodmin?'

'You're as bad as the rest of them, seeing harm that don't exist. I know my little girl...'

'Forgive my asking, but do you?'

Mrs Bodmin stood up. Her face was flushed.

'Look here, Mr Deene. I don't know who you are or what business any of this is of yours. But if you think Kenneth would ever have done anything to be ashamed of with a child like Liz you're very much mistaken.'

'I just wondered...'

'Well, don't. I suppose Connie Farnham's put you up to this. Asking all these questions. You ask *her* what the police told that thing she married before they made it legal, and see what she says to that.'

'I understood that her husband was a butcher.'

'So he is. Came in to the business from his uncle. That doesn't mean he doesn't hang round the public lavatory in the square every evening, does it? You can tell his wife—she's still his wife however much she may pretend to be with Ken's father—you can tell her to keep her nose out of my affairs.'

'But, Mrs Bodmin, there seems very little doubt that Kenneth, or Dutch as they call him, has been murdered. Have you anything to suggest about that?'

'Not unless it was her or Bert Carver that did it.'

'The boy's own father?'

'Now he's mixed up with *her* I'd put nothing past him.'

'You don't think it more likely to have been some of the young fellows in the town?'

'Well, there are these skinheads. From what you read about in the papers they might do anything. Look at that case the other day...'

'I'm more interested in this case, here and now. I want to get to the truth of it.'

'Well you won't if you listen to what Connie Farnham tells you, that's a sure thing.'

'Did Kenneth ride a motor-bike?' asked Carolus, seeking to divert Mrs Bodmin from the subject of Connie Farnham.

'Not lately he hasn't. He smashed his own bike up about three months ago and since then he generally seems to ride behind one of the other lads. Especially one of the two that had long hair same as his. The three of them were always about together, Des Grayne and young Phil White. They both had bikes and Ken would ride on the back of them. But not one of his own he hadn't, not for a long time.'

'What sort of lads are they, these two?'

'Just ordinary. Same as they all are nowadays. That's as far as I know. I don't see a lot of people in the town because I work in the Canteen at the Plastics Factory and that means pretty long hours. I'm only here today because it's my day off.'

'So my little friend Liz manages to look after herself, I take it?'

'She's a handy little thing. She can do anything about the house. She's only twelve you know. Since I lost my husband from a heart attack he had at the Works I've had to Go Out, you see. But Liz is quite safe to be left on her own. Of course she's at school all day. I never asked you if you'd like a cup of tea? I'm just going to put the kettle on, if you feel like it.'

'Thank you very much. I'm so glad you speak well of Kenneth Carver. I began to think no one had a good word to say for him.'

'I'll tell you who else will have.'

'His mother?'

'Not *her*. She'd never have a good word to say for anyone except herself. No, Mr Leng. He's the organist in the church here. You'll find him a very nice fellow and he took quite an interest in Kenneth. He's the choirmaster, too. Mind you, he doesn't need to do it because he's got plenty of money. His father left it him. But he likes playing the organ and that. Him and his wife are ever so good with the young people. I should think he's the only one around here that took any interest in Kenneth. His parents certainly didn't.'

'I must go and see him,' decided Carolus.

'That's right. He lives in that old house you see at

the top of the hill by the church. Only his wife's been away for a few weeks, I believe. She may be back now. She has a sister living in France and pops across every now and then. But anyway he'll be there all right. Tell him Mrs Bodmin told you to ask about Kenneth. He'll tell you there was a lot of good in the boy.'

'Thank you, Mrs Bodmin.'

'You must stay and have that cup of tea. It's just ready.'

Over tea Carolus asked Mrs Bodmin when was the last time she had seen Kenneth.

'Oh not for a week or more,' she said. 'I daresay Liz has seen him since then only she may not remember. Of course I haven't told her what's happened to Kenneth—Dutch she calls him. She was ever so fond of him and I don't want to upset her. It upset me, I can tell you. When I first heard he'd been found over near Newminster lying in a gutter with not a stitch on, I thought whatever will happen next?'

'It was very startling. And nobody seems to have a clue about it, except that it looks as though he'd been taken there on the pillion of a motor-cycle.'

'Yes. So I heard. That may have been just to get rid of the body, mayn't it? But I can't think why anyone should want to do such a thing. Of course Des and Phil aren't the only ones to have motor-bikes. All that skinhead lot have them and make no end of noise racing up and down the streets at night. Might have been anyone, so far as that goes. All I can say is I hope you find out about it. I really do.'

So Carolus thanked Mrs Bodmin for the tea and went out to his car. He felt he had done pretty well for the first day, though he had not a glimpse of anything definite yet.

He decided not to stay in Hartington but to telephone Mrs Stick to expect him in Newminster where he could think things over in the comfort of his own house. There was something ugly about Hartington—and not only about the various small factories and council houses. An ugly spirit, he thought, malicious and jealous. He would be glad to be away from the place in the hours of darkness.

Mrs Stick greeted him rather disapprovingly.

'There's only scraps for dinner,' she said, 'you having told me you didn't expect to be back.'

Carolus was inclined to rate as rather better than scraps the Sole Mornay and cold Guinea-fowl, (Pint a dew to Mrs Stick) which his housekeeper produced for him, but he only smiled approval.

'Mr Gorringer's just rung up,' said Mrs Stick when she brought Carolus's coffee. 'He wanted to know if you were back so I had to tell him. He's coming round in half-an-hour he says.'

'Thank you, Mrs Stick. Don't wait up if you want to go to bed.'

'Not yet I don't. Stick's quite taken to the telly since you gave us the coloured one, sir. He doesn't seem to like to leave it at night.'

In less than the time he had anticipated he heard Mr Gorringer's ring at the bell and in a few moments the Headmaster had joined him by the fire.

'Well, Deene. So it's once more into the breach, dear friends. I hear you are engaged in a new investigation?'

'True. I want to find out who murdered the youth found by Stick on the Boxley Road.'

'I glanced at the details in the *Newminster Gazette* this morning,' admitted Mr Gorringer. 'A sordid affair it seems.'

'All murders are sordid,' retorted Carolus.

'I do not deny it. But I cannot help wondering sometimes why you are so deeply interested in them, in that case.'

'Perhaps you have a point there,' said Carolus rather wearily. 'Did you know that Hollingbourne had the boy as a paying guest some years ago?'

'Impossible, surely, Deene. The boy was of the artisan class, I gathered.'

'Hollingbourne explained to me that the boy's father, who is a factory foreman, could afford to get rid of his son for a time and Mrs Hollingbourne accepted him into her family circle. They regretted it.'

'I should think so. Did the boy give much trouble?'

'You must ask Hollingbourne. At all events the poor little wretch is dead and no one but one young detective named Grimsby seems to be much interested in the matter.'

'So you are drawn to investigate. You do not, I hope, forget the fact that term begins in three weeks' time?'

Carolus smiled. 'There is plenty of time to win this game and thrash the ... Upper Fifth too.'

'I perceive you are being frivolous, Deene. We abandoned corporal punishment several years ago. Have you any theory about the case in hand?'

'None yet,' said Carolus. 'I only started my enquiries today.'

'I see. They will doubtless take you into murky waters. A boy of barely sixteen murdered, it would seem, by ruffians scarcely older than him.'

'I've no idea who murdered the boy,' said Carolus. 'I certainly have not accepted as yet the theory, current in Hartington, that other youths were guilty.'

'But you haven't rejected it?'

'No. I haven't begun to consider more than vaguely.'

'Ah well. We know your methods. I've no doubt dawn will break before long. In the meantime let us discuss the coming term. You are, I believe, to tackle the Corn Laws with the Upper Fifth. A fascinating subject.'

'Do you think so? I always found it a bore at school. Have a drink, Headmaster?'

'Thank you, Deene. A suggestion of your excellent brandy.'

Carolus poured out a good two fingers and Mr Gorringer sipped appreciatively.

'I trust,' he said, 'that you will allow me to collaborate in some small measure if the situation demands it?'

'Thank you. I will keep you informed.'

Pleased with that assurance Mr Gorringer soon afterwards took his leave.

Chapter Five

Next day Carolus planned to call first on the dead
boy's mother and then to see the choirmaster Warton
Leng. But when he arrived at the house where Estelle
Carver lived with Justus Delafont, who had been vari-
ously described as a 'West Indian' 'a Jamaican' and 'an
African' he rang in vain at the front door. After a
few moments a window in the house next door was
opened.

'She's down at the Maison Chic,' said a female voice.
'Having her hair done. Did you want something?'

'Just a few words with Mrs Carver,' Carolus explained.

The woman next door who was youngish and smiled
easily, said, 'Delafont, she calls herself now. You better
not say Carver. She doesn't like that. Though every-
body knows what her real name is.'

'Thanks for the advice,' said Carolus.

'Who shall I say called?' When Carolus did not
immediately answer, the neighbour supplied sugges-
tions. 'Was it about the hire purchase?' she asked. 'I
know she meant to pay it this week. Or are you from
the Health Insurance people? It can't be about her
mother's pension again. She only settled all that last
month. If it's those books that were left here she

doesn't want them. She said you were to take them away if you came. Or have you come about her son being found dead? She says she's not going to talk about that if anyone asks.'

'I think I had better come back later,' said Carolus.

'She'll want to know who it was,' the neighbour said. 'Unless you're from the Union? If so you'd better see Mr Delafont and he won't be home till this evening. You can't be the Jehovah's Witnesses because they always come in pairs. I know she's paid for the milk up to last week. I must tell her something.'

'Just tell her a Mr Deene called and will come back this afternoon,' said Carolus.

'All right. I will. She'll be home some time this morning. She's only gone to have her hair done, like she does every Thursday. Only she's going to have a change this week, she told me. More round the back of the head.'

'Quite,' said Carolus.

'She's a good customer to Mr Barnet, that's who keeps the Maison Chic. She takes a lot of notice of her appearance. Always has done, ever since I've known her.'

Carolus smiled and moved towards his car.

'I'll tell her you've been,' the neighbour called after him.

'Thank you.'

'She'll be home all the afternoon, as far as I know.'

'Good.'

Carolus got safely into his car. He fancied as he started the engine that the neighbour's voice was still faintly audible.

'He lives in that old house you see on the hill by the church,' Mrs Bodmin had said of Warton Leng, but Carolus had not stopped to make enquiries of Mrs

Carver's neighbour, guessing that it would mean a
long delay. He drove on and found a house which
answered to the description. He thought as he examined its red brick front and eight-paned windows
that it was a charming piece of eighteenth-century
architecture to find surrounded by the ugly modern
dwellings which made up most of Hartington.

The door was opened by a neat little Sam Weller
of a man with a polishing cloth in his hand.

'Mr Leng?' Carolus asked.

'No. I'm his friend Skilly,' said the man.

'Could I see Mr Leng?'

'I expect you could. He's in his study. This way.'

Mr Skilly opened a door and said—'Warton, someone to see you!' Then left Carolus to go in.

Carolus found Warton Leng a benevolent-looking
individual in his fifties, that was to say some ten years
older than Carolus judged Skilly.

'I know all about you,' Leng greeted Carolus.
'You're trying to find out who was responsible for the
death of poor young Carver. I'll do anything I can to
help you.'

'Thanks,' said Carolus. 'Most of the other inhabi-
tants of this town seem to think I'm wasting my time.
Either that or they practically say it was a good rid-
dance.'

'I know,' said Leng. 'He wasn't popular. He came
from what the more sanctimonious of muck-rakers
call "a broken home".'

'But you befriended the boy?'

'Or exploited him. I don't know quite which. He
had a fine voice. But he went about with a rotten
crowd of layabouts.'

'Des Grayne and Phil White,' supplied Carolus.

'Not only those two. He seemed to know all the young blackguards in Hartington.'

'But not the so-called skinheads surely?'

'I don't know about that. There was a fellow named Bodmin who belonged to that lot...'

Carolus managed to nod carelessly. He had no intention of using Mrs Bodmin's introduction to Leng. 'What about him?' he asked.

'A particularly unpleasant young villain. He had it in for Dutch.'

'They all had, so I've heard.'

'But this one, Gil Bodmin, particularly. He was the cousin of a small girl...'

'Liz,' said Carolus quietly.

'You seem to know more than I can tell you.'

'I had never heard of this character. But the name can't be usual. I've been to see Mrs Bodmin.'

'Yes, that's his aunt. But Mrs Bodmin will have nothing to say to her lout of a nephew. She told poor Dutch to keep the little girl away from him and I'm sure he did.'

'Do you think that Gil's anger and spite at that was sufficient to get his crowd to work on Dutch?'

'I shouldn't think so. I know Gil had a lot of influence with the others. But there was nothing, that I know of, which actually suggests that the skinheads were responsible for Dutch's death. If there was you wouldn't have much difficulty in narrowing down your enquiries, but I think it would be a great mistake to suspect them just because they are so-called skinheads.'

'I agree,' said Carolus. 'I should find any sort of guess at this point most dangerous. Besides, I have not even seen these famous skinheads yet.'

'They use a pub called the Dragon chiefly.'

'They drink then? By all accounts that's a healthier

taste than those of the long-haired boys who go in for pot.'

Leng smiled.

'I can see you're not very experienced in this sort of thing. Delinquency, I mean, not crime.'

'Are you?'

'I make it my business to know something about it.'

'As a choirmaster?'

'Well, yes. If you want to know. Skinheads and Greasers, as the Press call them, can't be divided into two completely opposing factions. They have certain things in common. Some greasers take pot, some skinheads drink. But some of each do the other, if you see what I mean. Gil Bodmin, I believe, does both.'

'What about your protégé, Dutch Carver?'

'I don't think he took pot. He may have had a pint occasionally.'

'You knew him really well?'

'I had known him for a long time. Can one say one knows any of these youngsters well, nowadays?'

'You agree with Mrs Bodmin—he wasn't a bad boy?'

'I do. Yet—to be frank—I cannot pretend to have been altogether surprised when I heard the news.'

'You mean, in an expressive idiom, he stuck his neck out?'

'Something like that. We live in an age of violence.'

'I see you don't mean to tell me what *are* your suspicions,' said Carolus.

'I have none. I'm entirely at sea.'

'The police theory, I gather,' said Carolus, 'is that he was killed on the Saturday afternoon or evening and taken over to be dumped by the Boxley Road near Newminster during the night of Saturday. There were marks on his wrists and ankles that suggest he was carried on the pillion seat of a motor-cycle, either unconscious or dead.'

'So I understand.'

'Doesn't *that* make you suspect the skinheads?'

'Not necessarily. It could have been one of his own crowd with whom he had fallen out. And his brother rides a motor-bike. We're looking to you to decide that.'

'I shall do my best. You don't know of anyone who saw Dutch on the Saturday?'

'Yes. My friend Skilly. Dutch came here at about two o'clock on Saturday afternoon. He asked for me but Skilly told him I'd gone up to town to meet my wife. He seemed surprised at that because I usually go up on Friday. It was an exception for me to go on Saturday. Skilly asked him to come in but he didn't wait. He told Skilly the repairs on his motor-bike were finished and he was going to get it from the garage.'

'He was on foot, then?'

'Yes, he smashed his motor-bike up some weeks ago.'

'That doesn't get us much farther, does it? He walked out of your front gate and from then till Sunday when my gardener Stick found his body in a ditch by the Boxley Road we know nothing of his movements. Or if he had any.'

Leng was thoughtful.

'Do you know that road?' he asked.

'Of course. I come by it to Hartington—whenever I come to Hartington, which frankly isn't often. Why?'

'It's dark and pretty deserted. But I shouldn't have thought it was an ideal site for a murder.'

'I see what you mean,' said Carolus.

'This thing has shaken me,' said Leng. 'Thank heavens my wife is back.'

'What did she think of the boy?'

'What we all did, I suppose. That he had a fine voice but was in many ways a young fool. I think she was quite fond of him in a way. We have no children of our own.'

'And Mr Skilly?'

'He's my wife's cousin. As a matter of fact I met her through him. He's a very old friend. Lives with us here. I don't think he had much opinion one way or the other about Dutch Carver. He's chiefly interested in this house and garden. Domesticated type.'

'I see. Well, Mr Leng, I am sure you will let me know if anything occurs to you which might help me find out the truth.'

'I certainly will. Though of course I shall tell the police, too.'

'Of course. They depend more than me on their technical knowledge of this sort of crime. Forensic chemistry and so on. I have to trust to my instincts.'

'I've always got on pretty well with the police. I had to work with them during the War. I was in Field Security, you see.'

'Were you? I was in a far less exciting outfit. Commandos. It seems a long time ago now.'

As Leng showed him out of the front door Carolus noticed a Daimler, of a violent yellow colour, in the stable yard. It had not been visible from the drive by which he had come in.

'By George,' he said, with professional interest. 'Is that your car?'

'Yes. Bit of a screamer, isn't it?'

'I like strong colours on cars, though mine's black.'

'Skilly's the same. He says he approves of mine but has a quiet little green Cortina for himself.'

Carolus said goodbye, and as an afterthought asked

Leng if he might come again if there was anything else he wanted to know.

'Of course,' Leng said. 'Come in any time.'

Now it was time for Dutch Carver's mother and Carolus reminded himself to say 'Mrs Delafont' when he addressed her.

She had seemingly dressed for the occasion for surely a busy housewife would not be likely to be wearing what could only be described as a tea-gown, if such a thing was possible in the 1970's. She welcomed Carolus and explained rather archly that she could guess what he had come about.

'You want to tell me about the Investment Trust I wrote in about.'

'No,' said Carolus, but at first it did not seem that Estelle Delafont, as Flo Carver had become, had heard him. She was examining herself with a broad smile of approval in the mirror over the mantelpiece.

'I was sorry I was out when you came this morning. I was having my hair done. Do you like it?'

'No,' said Carolus determined to attract her full attention, and before she could speak added—'I've come to see you about your son Kenneth, the one who has been murdered.'

He pronounced the last word with such emphasis that Estelle looked positively alarmed.

'I did see something in the paper about it,' she answered coolly.

'You know you *had* a son, presumably?' went on Carolus. 'And that on Sunday night he was found dead in a ditch beside the road, stark naked?'

'I don't know anything about that,' said Estelle.

'You know now, because I've just told you. I gather Kenneth was not your favourite son. But surely news like this must be painful to you?'

'I suppose it is. Of course I hadn't seen much of him lately. Are they sure it was murder?'

'Quite sure. He had been suffocated.'

'Dreadful, isn't it? Would you care for a cup of tea?'

'No thanks. When did you see him last?'

'Who? Kenneth? Oh not for a long time. My husband didn't encourage him to come here.'

'Your...?'

'Mr Delafont. He had no use for Kenneth. He knew how he'd made me suffer.'

'How?'

'He was always a thoughtless boy. Not like his brother Roger. Even his father admits that. I was so ashamed when he—Kenneth I mean—got into all that trouble.'

'What trouble?'

'He was never out of it. The police and everything. People looked at me as though it was my fault, as though I hadn't brought him up properly. I'm sure I did everything I could for him. Mr Delafont says I did far too much.'

'And did you?'

'At first I did. But when I saw that he had no gratitude at all I gave it up. If you can't show a little appreciation, I said, you can get someone else to do things for you because I'm not going to. Mr Delafont said I was quite right. I don't like the way he's made it all curl up above the ears, do you?'

Carolus, who had long practise in this kind of dialogue, was able to realize that it had switched to this morning's session at the Maison Chic but hung on like a bull-dog to the subject of Kenneth.

'How long is it, would you say, since you had helped your younger son?'

'Helped him? He doesn't need help! He's always got plenty of money, and buys himself more new clothes than I can afford to. Sometimes I think I look almost *shabby*. Don't you think so?'

'I don't know anything about it. Did you see Kenneth on the Saturday afternoon before his body was found?'

'Well, I don't know about seeing him. The lady next door who spoke to you this morning did mention that he'd been round early in the afternoon.'

'How early?'

'Before three, she said. I had the telly on and didn't know anything about it. She said he didn't hardly touch the bell of the front door but that he went away again. I didn't hear it and it's a good thing I didn't because I'd have told him to clear off, pretty quick. I've got too much to look after without bothering about him.'

'Did anyone bother about Kenneth, Mrs Delafont?'

'Well, it was his own fault. He never paid any attention to me so I seemed to lose interest in him. Do you like these shoes? I bought them this morning at the Co-Op. It's the style nowadays. Only it changes so quickly you never know where you are.'

Carolus was silent and Kenneth's mother said—'Well, I must Get On. I've got a lot to do before Mr Delafont comes home. I hope you're successful,' she added insincerely. 'It's a nasty thing to have come on suddenly like that. Do you happen to know what they'll do about the funeral? I should think the police would look after that, wouldn't you? They've done it all so far. I mean they wouldn't expect his father and me to be responsible, would they? Not after what's happened. There's one thing, though. Whatever do you think happened to his clothes? It seems funny his having been found with nothing on. Do you think someone did it so they wouldn't recognize him? Or was it out of spite? You read of that, don't you, only it's usually a woman they do it to. It must have given someone a start, finding him like that. Only you can't tell nowadays. You never know what you're going to see in the papers next. Well, ta ta, then. I hope you get to the truth of all this. It quite upsets me when I think of it. Only Mr Delafont says I mustn't worry. Things like this are always happening.'

She waved gaily from the door and Carolus escaped.

Chapter Six

'The Dragon', Leng had named as the pub used by the skinheads, and Carolus made for it. He left his car in a more or less concealed park and entered the bar-room.

It was empty but for two youths unmistakably of the kind he expected to find. One was a tall hefty young man with a rather brutish expression on his face, the other a skinnier individual with small cunning eyes.

Carolus went straight up to them. He expected trouble and did not mean to leave them the initiative. He was fit, remarkably fit for his age, but knew something of the modern idea of fair odds in a fight.

'Either of you named Bodmin?' he asked.

They did not turn towards him or make any direct answer but the bigger youth turned to his shifty friend and asked in a tired voice, 'Who's this mug?'

The friend obliged. 'Some mug,' he answered, not very inventively.

The larger oaf continued still addressing his friend—'Looks like the Law to me. They get them in all sizes nowadays.'

The friend grinned. 'But not this sort, surely.'

Carolus did not show any anger.

'I asked you a question,' he said to the taller one.

'And I didn't answer. So push off, will you? We're talking.'

Carolus without any haste or excitement, picked up the youth's newly filled pint of beer and emptied it over his head. There was a splutter, a lunge and in a second the youth was on the floor.

The friend made no attempt to go to his assistance. He seemed baffled.

'How did you do that?' he asked Carolus. 'Karate?'

'Nothing so oriental,' Carolus replied. 'Just old-fashioned Unarmed Combat which we learned in the last war.' The big boy had struck his head on something and looked up dazed.

Carolus extended a hand.

'Ups-a-daisy,' he said good-humouredly. 'And the next question I ask will be answered. Is your name Gil Bodmin?'

'What about it?'

'Where were you on the Saturday night when Dutch Carver was murdered?'

'Nowhere in particular. Why? I had nothing to do with it!'

'You are deplorably bad at answering questions. I asked you where you were that night?'

'You were at the Cattle Market, weren't you Gil? That's a discotheque,' suggested the skinny one.

'That's right,' agreed Gil.

'Did you see anything of Dutch Carver?'

'No. I didn't. I never saw him that day, or the day before.'

'Or the day after?'

'Course not. He was dead, wasn't he?'

'You tell me.'

'Everyone says so, anyway. He was supposed to have

been done on the Saturday night. And found over near
Newminster on Sunday.'

'How do you think he got there?'

'I don't know! How am I to know? I never saw him.
What do you want to ask me for?'

'He doesn't know anything about it,' put in the
friend.

'Had you got anything against Dutch Carver?'

'No. Only that he was a greaser. Not one of our
crowd. I didn't do him, if that's what you mean.'

'Then I wonder why so many people in Hartington
seem to think you did.'

'I can't help what they think. I never touched him.'

'You have a motor-cycle?'

'Yes. So have all the other lads.'

'Was Dutch ever on your pillion?'

'No!' Gil shouted. 'Never! I wouldn't take a greaser
like that on my pillion. Or have anything to do with
him.'

'Or cut his hair?'

'Who cut his hair? I didn't. I didn't know anything about that. If someone cut his hair off it wasn't
me.'

'But it might have been, Gil? I mean you or some
of your friends have been known to cut off long hair
from what you call the greasers, haven't you?'

'Not me. Some of them have. Well, they're such
——ing cissies with hair half down their back. Some
of the lads don't like to see it.' He turned on his
friend. 'Tell him about the cushion,' he said.

'It's only that they're stuffing a cushion with the
greasers' hair. Like Indians with scalps. Not Gil, mind
you. Some of the other lads.'

Carolus had to be content with that information, at
least for the moment.

'Now you answer me some questions,' suggested Gil, whose courage seemed to be regained. 'Are you the Law?'

'No. Just a private individual, but interested,' said Carolus. 'Why doesn't your aunt want you to have anything to do with her little daughter?'

'Who says she doesn't? She's never taken any interest in young Liz herself. Leaves her to run about the streets all day. Then she tells you I have to keep away from her.'

'Why?' persisted Carolus.

'I don't know why. Because she's an old bitch, I suppose. She'd sooner let that greaser take her about than what she would me. What the kid needs is her mother to look after her.'

'Your aunt seems to work very hard.'

'No more than anyone else. And she doesn't need to. She's got a pension from my Uncle Jack.'

'We're getting away from the subject. You say you had nothing to do with Dutch's death. Who do you suggest might have, then?'

'Almost anybody. No one liked him. Even his brother had no use for him. And the rest of his greaser friends—Grayne and White and all that lot. You should have heard them talk about him. They're supposed to have said they meant to do for him one day ...'

'To whom did they say that?'

'I don't know. That's what I heard, anyway. I wouldn't put it past his own father for that matter. Or that bitch he's living with.'

'What about his mother?'

Gil grinned.

'Have you *seen* her?' he asked. 'But I never liked that Pakistani fellow ...'

'Not Pakistani, surely? I understand that Delafont is a West Indian.'

'So he may be, but I don't like the look of him. There's one, if you're looking for who did Dutch. Could easily have been him. And I'll tell you who else may have had something to do with it. That's the fellow who owns the discotheque where the greasers go. Swindleton he's called. Just the type. Mind you, I don't say it *was* him, but I wouldn't be a bit surprised. Dutch was always round there. Wasn't he, Trimmer?'

'Trimmer' was evidently the skinny friend.

'Certainly was,' he replied. 'Never came anywhere where we went.'

'What about girls?'

Gil grinned again.

'What about them?'

'You talk as though yours was an all-male community, and Dutch's crowd, too.'

'Oh yes. There were girls all right. Only ours didn't seem to mix much with theirs. There was some seemed to go for the greasers, like that Lotta.'

'Lotta?'

'Yeh. Carlotta her name is. A big busty girl. Always round with Jenny Rivers. They might be able to tell you something about Dutch. They went to the Spook Club, too. Lotta works in the same place as my sister. King's Supermarket. She's nearly always on the vegetables if you go round there. Big girl, she is. Always got a grin on her face. My sister's a cashier. Gets more money and shorter hours.'

Carolus for the first time became aware of the man behind the bar. He wore a fancifully trimmed beard and seemed to be listening intently to the conversation without wishing to interrupt it.

'Have a drink?' Carolus asked the two young men, thinking that they had been quite long enough on the premises without showing themselves as customers. They both accepted bitter, and Carolus asked for pints and a Scotch for himself. They were all served and Gil turned to Carolus in almost a friendly way.

'Cheers,' he said. 'Tell you what. Are you going to show me that trick of yours? How you put me down, I mean? Quickest thing I ever saw. And you say it's not Karate?'

'It's easy,' said Carolus and repeated his original performance but less violently.

Gil took it well and got to his feet.

'Try it on *him*,' he said indicating Trimmer. 'I want to watch.'

Trimmer was a willing victim.

'Unarmed Combat, you say,' put in the landlord. 'Looks to me more like Jiu-Jitsu.'

He was interrupted by the entrance of a group of shaven-headed louts who gave surly greetings to Gil and Trimmer.

Carolus saw that an extraordinary change had come over Gil. All his good humour disappeared and his face took on the bestial expression it had worn when Carolus arrived. It was evident that he had what in other circles might have been called 'a position to keep up'. It would never do for him to be seen by his friends or followers or whatever the new arrivals were, in polite conversation with Carolus.

Carolus could understand that. He knew enough about these street gangs to know that leadership could only be maintained by a show of vicious, often criminal, strength. But it was a revelation of the young man's character.

'Ought to have seen Gil just now,' said Trimmer who

was evidently less aware than Carolus was of the subtlety of the situation.

'Why?' said a dark-haired boy who, Carolus learned afterwards, was named Nat Fisher.

This seemed to release a spring in Gil.

'Shut up!' he shouted to Trimmer, moving towards him.

'Ought to have seen him!' continued Trimmer derisively. He got no further. With startling speed Gil had produced a knife and was holding it under Trimmer's chin.

'I told you to shut up,' he said furiously.

Trimmer was—quite literally and obviously—afraid for his life.

'I was only saying,' he muttered.

'Next time I tell you to shut up,' Gil said, 'you shut up. And quick. Now get going and don't let me see you again.'

Trimmer turned by the door.

'I wasn't going to say anything,' he said.

Gil did not seem to find this worth answering but Trimmer's departure was delayed by the landlord.

'You owe me for that first round.'

Thus brought back into the room Trimmer became almost effusive.

'So I do. Must have forgotten. How much was it?'

The landlord told him and Trimmer brought out a pound note.

'Out!' said Gil when the landlord had given him his change.

Gil's prestige was restored and Carolus was left alone with four of the town's skinheads and observed their movements.

'Who's this ——?' demanded Nat Fisher after a seemingly contemptuous glance at Carolus.

'Some bloke,' said Gil. The fact that he used a less offensive term than Nat seemed to indicate to the others that Gil did not find Carolus's presence unwelcome.

'D'you know him?' Nat asked the landlord.

'Never seen him before,' said the bearded man behind the bar. 'He's pretty good at...'

'D'you want what Trimmer's got coming to him?' Gil asked, leaning threateningly across the bar.

The landlord was not as scared as Trimmer had been, but he was scared. A noteworthy force seemed to be represented by Gil Bodmin.

'I was only going to say he was pretty good at darts,' said the landlord with considerable presence of mind.

Carolus had been amused that all this talk referring to him had been carried on as though he was not present, or perhaps in existence. None of the youths seemed to be of quite normal intelligence though Gil was the least primitive of them all. He could well see how they had become the chief suspects in the case of Dutch Carver's death though he had seen nothing positively murderous about any of them, except perhaps Gil's schizophrenic determination to dominate the situation at all costs. That, Carolus realized, could indeed be dangerous. Suppose that Dutch Carver had called down upon himself some of that brutal violence, that consuming vanity of a youth who precariously held on to his authority over the others, would it not have meant just what Dutch had suffered, gross humiliation and death? It was no use turning back to the time of awkward young ruffians, mischievous boys, the unruly sons of weak parents—these boys were potential killers. Not one of them, not even the shifty

Trimmer, could be erased from a list of suspects in the case.

On the other hand there were people as likely to have been involved as these, and Carolus remembered the two abominable parents on whom he was inclined to lay the blame for what Dutch had become. And he had yet to meet the sinister Swindleton and the two girls whom Gil had connected with Dutch.

As though prompted to action by these thoughts Carolus rose. Out of consideration for Gil he refrained from speaking to anyone and with a nod to the land-lord left the pub. Four motor-cycles were drawn up outside like chorus boys waiting for their turn.

When he reached the car park where he had put his car out of sight of those entering, he was surprised to see Gil waiting for him. He had evidently come out by the back door of the pub, perhaps leaving his friends with an excuse or perhaps not bothering to explain himself.

'This your barrow?' asked Gil.

Carolus said yes.

The boy looked embarrassed and shame-faced. He did not seem able to speak for some minutes then he came out with the sudden remark, 'I didn't kill Dutch,' and was again silent.

'Do you know who did?' Carolus asked calmly.

'I may have got an idea.'

'Well?'

'Nothing to go on. I can't really say anything at all. Only if I was you I shouldn't look among the youngsters like us.'

'Someone older, you think?'

'I'm not going to say anything because I don't know. But if I was you that's where I should look.'

'Not among your lot?' suggested Carolus.

'I'm not saying some of us wouldn't have liked to. But I'm pretty sure it wasn't. It took more than thinking he was a ——ing greaser to bring anyone to that. Someone must have had more reason than what any of us had. See what I mean?'

'Vaguely, yes. I shall get at the truth anyway. It may take a bit of time ...'

'What about the Law? Don't you think they'll beat you to it?'

'Shouldn't think so. I'm learning all the time.'

'Learn anything this evening?' asked Gil.

'Quite a lot. You don't cover up very well, Gil.'

'I don't know. Anyway, I've got nothing to cover up.'

'No?'

'Another thing. You have a look at that Swindleton. If you don't get something out of him himself you'll learn a lot from his place, the Spook Club.'

'Thanks,' said Carolus.

'There's a girl there called ...'

From across the yard someone was shouting—'Gil! Come on Gil, we're pushing off.'

'Shall have to run,' Gil said. 'See you again some time.'

'What was the girl called?'

'June!' called Gil from a few yards away. 'June Mockett.'

He dived under the railing of the car park and could be heard swearing amicably at his friends near the back door.

Chapter Seven

Carolus was not superstitious and was not greatly troubled by what Mrs Stick called 'the creeps' 'the shivers' or 'a turn'. But somehow that evening when he went to drive back to Newminster by the road beside which he had found, guided by Stick, the body of the boy known as Dutch, he was filled with uncomfortable presentiments. It was a cold windy night, for one thing, one of those autumnal nights on which the trees seemed to be moved by angry unrest and their noise by the side of the road sounded like animals trying to break out rather than the placid vegetation, which all through the summer had given shade. Twice on his way he stopped the car to listen to this, not in any ordinary sense frightened but thinking that on such a night the dark landscape seemed to be alive about him.

The case he was investigating was not one which carried threats or any articulate kind of horror, but there was a morbidness and a cruelty about it which perturbed him. No one cared anything for the young boy who had been killed, even Leng, Carolus thought, showed only a professional interest in Dutch Carver as a singer and seemed to have no time to spare for him as a human being. Herbert Carver, nagged if not domi-

nated by the Farnham woman, made it clear that he
wanted to be troubled as little as possible by what
should have been to him a tragic event, while the
silly vain mother of the boy, in a modern phrase,
couldn't have cared less. Even the investigating policeman confessed that he had not long been in the CID
and that he was being given his first opportunity to
find out the truth about a murder.

Altogether, Carolus decided, it looked like being
one of those cases which barely attained newspaper
space and would soon be swept under the forensic
carpet. He was quite alone in being determined not
to let that happen.

After he had passed through Boxley and was approaching the very stretch of road by the side of which
Stick had indicated the body of Dutch, he half decided
to pull up again and have another look at the place.
What possible object this could serve he did not know.
All traces of the incident had long since disappeared
and skilled police examiners had been over the ground
which had since been exposed to the weather. Yet
there was a sort of fascination in the idea, perhaps
like that mysterious fascination to murderers which is
supposed to attract them to the scene of their crime.

He was about to dismiss this as absurd and to
accelerate when he became aware of something real
but inexplicable. On the grass verge, across which
by his own account Stick had been rudely pushed by a
car, Carolus saw an object—or was it a creature? At all
events the shape of a man lying full length. Carolus
pulled up short so that his headlights shone towards
whatever it was that attracted his attention. Was it a
man or no more than an artfully arranged bundle of
rags, a sort of prone scarecrow? At all events nearby
lying on its side was a motor-cycle.

Carolus felt sure, sitting there staring at these, that the two objects were not the result of an accident. The man had not been thrown from the saddle of his motor-bike, the motor-bike was not lying there after a crash. They were altogether too deliberately placed. It would be too much of a coincidence if of all the roads in England this particular one, and this particular length of it had been the scene of a crash within ten days of the finding of Dutch Carver's dead body.

Yet what in heaven's name was the idea? The trees about him were torn by the wind and Carolus felt an almost irresistible urge to get out of the car and go to examine what he could see. His hand was on the door handle when it suddenly occurred to him, with a force much stronger than his own curiosity, that this—getting out of the car and going to whatever was lying there—was exactly what he was intended to do, that the whole thing was an elaborate trap, baited by the sight which had aroused his interest as it was meant to do. Who would not go to the assistance of a fallen motor-cyclist beside the road? He would need to be a Levite with an extraordinarily thick skin to pass by on the other side.

Still he hesitated then backed his car and drove it forward so that the lights fell exactly on the prone figure. Then suddenly, after watching a moment, he drove away, accelerating with all the force of his engine. He did not look back but covered some three miles at speed, till he was approaching a roundabout he knew.

Here, still maintaining a fair speed, he swerved round the circle and started following the road by which he had just come. He was not surprised to find that at the point where a man had lain beside a motor-bike there was nothing at all to be seen. Rider and motor-bike had completely disappeared.

Carolus did not attempt pursuit. It would be useless and he knew that between here and Boxley there were several by-roads and forks. Besides, an idea was growing in his mind that he knew the identity of the rider and with that knowledge he would be in a fair way to discover who had killed Dutch Carver. He decided to drive on to Newminster.

At home Mrs Stick was waiting up for him.

'Stick remembers where he saw that young man before,' she announced with no preliminaries.

Carolus obligingly asked where.

'He came into the Star one night some weeks ago. Stick remembers because the Star isn't the house he usually goes to because he never liked the People that had it, only they left some months ago and now some New People have got it and Stick thinks they're all right only they're very strict about who they serve. Anyhow this young fellow who was lying dead in the ditch the other night came in with some girl he'd picked up...'

Carolus interrupted, finding Mrs Stick too uncharitable in her judgments and phrases.

'How do you *know* he'd picked her up?' he demanded.

'You could Tell,' said Mrs Stick. 'I mean, it was written all over her, Stick says. So the new landlord waited to hear what the young fellow would ask for and then said—"I'm sorry, son. We don't serve them here as young as you are." Stick says this fellow looked as though he was going to make trouble only the girl got hold of his arm and started whispering to him and the two of them walked out. I expect they went to the Bell; they'd serve anyone there. But these New People at the Star are very strict.'

'Did Stick recognize the girl?'

'He says he's seen her before. He feels quite sure of that. Only it won't come to him now. He'll tell you if it does. Then that fellow's been round again.'

'Which fellow?'

Mrs Stick was never willing to use any of the accepted terms for the police; to say 'a police officer' would have choked her, as indeed it would a great many people, while 'a copper' 'a rozzer' 'a flattie' 'a constable' 'a busy' 'a bluebottle' or 'a dick' would have seemed undignified, not towards the police but in her own manner of speaking.

'That fellow that came to see you about the murder,' she said at last.

'Oh, Detective Sergeant Grimsby,' said Carolus.

'That's him, whatever name he calls himself. He wanted to know where you were but of course I wouldn't tell him. I mean it's no business of his where you are, is it?'

Carolus smiled.

'You might have said I was over at Hartington,' he said. 'Though I expect he guessed, anyway.'

'He said he'd be back this evening. Though he said when I asked him that there was nothing in particular he wanted to see you about.'

Ten minutes later Grimsby arrived.

'I don't think your housekeeper likes me much,' he said when the two men were alone.

'I must apologize for Mrs Stick. She has been sorely tried by my interests. Policemen and criminals are about equally distasteful to her.'

'So they are to a good many people I'm afraid. How have you been getting on, Carolus?'

'Oh not bad. Someone meant to have a go at me tonight.'

'Where?' asked Grimsby sharply.

'At the point where Stick found the body. Quite a coincidence, wasn't it? Except that you and I have been long enough at this game to know that there *are* no coincidences.'

'What happened?'

'I was driving back from Hartington when I had a quite unaccountable urge to have another look at the place where Dutch Carver's body was found. But I didn't need that urge—I saw a man lying beside an overturned motor-bike on the verge in front of the very place.'

'Did you examine him?'

'No.'

'Why not?'

'Because that was exactly what I was meant to do. It was a trap—a clever one because almost anyone would have jumped out of his car to have a look before he had considered the consequences.'

'But you didn't?'

'I don't claim much credit for that. I backed the car so that the lights were full on the man's figure.'

'Recognize him?'

'No. But I saw two things about him. One was that he was wearing goggles, and two—though I'm not quite certain of this—that he had what looked suspiciously like a revolver in his hand. Something metallic anyway. I certainly was not going to hang around and find out. And I was right. I drove up to the roundabout and back along the road I had come by. When I reached the spot both the man and the motor-bike had gone.'

'You've no idea who it was?'

'No idea. Or at least none that I'm going to suggest to you. We agreed that I should tell you facts, not theories. This would be nothing but the wildest theory. Remember, the man ...'

'Sure it was a man?'

'No. Not at all sure. It was lying in a way that prevented one from guessing. I was going to say that It— if you like—was wearing goggles. I could not guess the sex.'

'Yet you appear to have guessed the identity?'

'That could be from another source altogether.'

'You know, Carolus, this won't do. You tell me of what you think was an attempt at an attack on you which fortunately did not come off. I'm enough of a conventionally-minded policeman to get out a notebook at information like that. There has been a murder, remember. Not just a crime puzzle in a book. A boy of sixteen or seventeen—even the parents can't name the age exactly—has been killed and now you coolly tell me that someone, probably the same murderer, tried to ...'

'No, no. I didn't say tried to kill me. As if he intended to have a go at doing so. Or so I think. I don't know.'

'And you refuse to tell me what are your suspicions?'

'If you were in my class at school, Grimsby, I'd tear a strip off you for inaccurate statements. I don't refuse to tell you my suspicions—I haven't any. Only the beginnings of a probably crazy guess. I'm not going to give you that to tear up. And don't start Quiz games. You know—"man or woman"? That sort of thing. Because I shan't answer.'

'In that case I cannot be responsible for your safety.'

'When have you ever been? I can look after my own safety ...'

'Now, now, gentlemen,' said the voice of Mr Gorringer who had entered quietly from the hall. 'You shouldn't argue, you know. I have felt myself responsible for the safety of Mr Deene over a good many years and I realize it is no light matter.'

'This is Detective Sergeant Grimsby, Headmaster.'

'I'm delighted to meet you,' said Mr Gorringer. 'May I ask what bone of contention you have between you?'

'A small one,' said Carolus. 'Whether the Arsenal's last goal last Saturday was a foul.'

Mr Gorringer looked suspiciously from one to the other, but realized that he had to be content with that obvious invention.

'I, on the other hand,' he said, 'came to see whether Mr Deene has made any progress in the investigation he is making. Term-time draws on apace and I am naturally anxious that he should be done with one of his interests before becoming absorbed—as I hope—by the other. What do you say, Deene? Are the handcuffs ready? Does the cell await its murderous inhabitant?'

Grimsby rose to his feet. Perplexed—as well he might be—by Mr Gorringer's ornate diction, he said a hasty good night and went out.

'I hope I have not offended your friend by showing too much levity in a grave situation,' said Mr Gorringer.

Carolus smiled.

'No. On the contrary, Headmaster. But I haven't got very far, I'm afraid. It's turning out to be a tough case.'

'Dear, dear. The staff meeting with which as you will remember we usually usher in a new term, will be in little more than two weeks and you, Deene, seem occupied, if one may put it like that, in gory details which, as I have repeatedly told you, might

well be left to such as the no doubt excellent young
man who has just left us.'

'Yes. He's capable enough. It's just that I think I am
more deeply interested.'

'Oh yes. I have no doubt of that. Though I cannot
imagine why you should be so. I took the liberty of
giving the outline of the case as so far revealed to
Mrs Gorringer, and she of course, was not slow in
voicing one of her inimitable *bons mots*.'

Carolus bowed to the inevitable.

'What was that?' he asked, trying to keep the weari-
ness out of his tone.

'It is a pity, she said, that the author of an American
best-selling novel has already used the perfect title
for this case—*The Naked and the Dead*.'

Mr Gorringer laughed heartily and in sympathy
Carolus could not avoid giving him a swift smile.

'More seriously she considers, on the strength of
details garnered from Mrs Hollingbourne, with whom
Mrs Gorringer does some modest shopping from time
to time, that this is a case of a Broken Home. The
unfortunate youth appears to have been cared for by
no one. But doubtless you are aware of that.'

'Yes,' admitted Carolus.

'What you may *not* be aware of, my dear Deene, is a
piece of information I myself have ...'

'Garnered?'

'Yes. Garnered, for you from a most unexpected
source. One of the parents, in fact, whom I met in the
High Street the other day ...'

'Who was that?' asked Carolus.

'Let him or her be nameless. It is a matter of confidence. But I am in a position to tell you that there is
in Hartington an institution called by the curious
name of a *discotheque*.'

'Which one?' asked Carolus.

'I understand that it is known by the ridiculous name of the Spook Club.'

'Oh yes,' said Carolus off-handedly and with the intention of riling the Headmaster. 'Swindleton's place.'

Mr Gorringer raised his hand to indicate that he had further details to impart.

'The proprietor, aptly named as you say, Swindleton, is believed to handle drugs, even to traffic in them among the young people who are foolish enough to patronize his ... *discotheque*, if I must use that odious misnomer.'

'He's a pusher, you mean? So I've heard. I have not met him yet.'

'Then do so with all haste, my dear Deene. I heard enough—in confidence as I've explained—to be certain that the man Swindleton exercises a corrupting influence in the town of Hartington. He should be laid by the heels at once.'

'Now that *is* the concern of the police,' said Carolus.

'I do not deny it. But surely you who are engaged in the education of the young, will not turn aside in a matter like this?'

'First things first,' said Carolus.

'My informant was able to tell me more. The man Swindleton previously carried on much the same nefarious business in the salubrious town of Brighton.'

'Not so salubrious if he was there.'

'He kept a Coffee-House named the Jamaica Inn, and in the words of the parent who told me this and was only just able to snatch her elder son from the man's clutches, quantities of the drug cannabis resin was obtainable there. He was even suspected—though not, it seems, by the police—of dealing in heroin.'

'Really? I can scarcely believe that a pusher of

heroin worked in Brighton without being discovered.'
'You would be right. My informant told me that
Swindleton was sentenced to six months imprisonment.
It seems that he was treated lightly as a first offender.'
'And now he's at it again?'
'So it would seem, on information which I, for one,
find not lightly to be dismissed.'
'Thank you, Headmaster. I shall certainly keep that
in mind.'

Chapter Eight

This was more the type he was used to, thought Carolus, as he sat facing Ronald Swindleton across a large ornate 'Director's' desk. This was the kind of creature, in and out of prison for mean and cowardly crimes, shifty-eyed, over-dressed and having an 'old-chap' kind of speech which made his conversation sickening. Carolus knew where he was, as the cliché goes, with men of Swindleton's type, knew that it was only a question of time before the *discothècaire* would be slapping him on the back or pawing him in some way in an excess of pretended confidence. Carolus meant to avoid such familiarity and so far as he could maintain his role of a private detective employed by persons unknown. It seemed to work wonders with Swindleton.

'I wish I could help you, old man,' he said offering Carolus a cigarette which was refused. 'The truth is I didn't know much about the lad. I believe he used to come to my joint from time to time, but so did a few hundred others.'

'So many? You must be doing very well.'

'Well, you know what I mean,' smiled Swindleton.

'Yes. I think I do. But it's not what you say,' said Carolus. 'Who were young Carver's associates?'

'I really couldn't say, off-hand. I daresay some of the

girls would know. I tell you what, I'll try to find out for you and give you the information in a few days' time. How would that do?'

'It wouldn't do at all,' said Carolus, without giving any explanation of why he was turning down this handsome offer.

'Can't do more than that,' Swindleton said, lifting his narrow shoulders in an elaborate shrug. 'We can't keep tabs on all our customers. After all, we don't *know* they're going to be murdered, do we? No one could have been more upset than me when I heard about Carver.'

'When did you hear?'

'Must have been the Tuesday or Wednesday after it happened. I was sitting here as I usually am at this time in the morning when young Des Grayne rushed in and asked if I'd heard about Dutch. Of course I asked what about Dutch, and he said "Been done, that's all. Taken for a ride. Now he's in the morgue over at Newminster." I thought he was trying to be funny at first. You know how these kids talk. Half American slang, or what they believe it is. So I told him not to be a bloody little fool.

'He said "Straight up, Ron. Dutch has had it. Stark bollock naked and dead as a door nail." '

'Are you sure he said "taken for a ride"?' asked Carolus.

'Yes. But that doesn't mean anything. Old-fashioned slang from American gangster films of the twenties and thirties. That's all he meant.'

'You don't think he was speaking more literally?'

'No. He wouldn't know anything about that.'

'He called you "Ron"?'

'Yeh. Well they all do. Kids do, nowadays. They all say "Ron". After all it's my name.'

'Is it?' said Carolus evenly. 'Was that the name you were convicted under?'

'What are you talking about? You can't say things like that, you know, whoever you are. I've never been convicted.'

'Brighton. 1969,' said Carolus.

'What do you want to bring that up for?' said Swindleton. 'How would you like it if someone raked up your past when you were trying to live it down? And anyhow, what's it got to do with Carver's death?'

'I don't know,' said Carolus. 'What *has* it?'

'Bloody nothing. And you know it. Carver was a kid like any other who came here some nights. Liked to dance. Talked to a few girls.'

'That's what I asked you—who were his associates? You said you would have to make enquiries.'

'So I shall. But it just occurs to me. There was one girl he saw a lot of—Jenny Rivers. He used to come in with her and stay with her all the evening. That's if June didn't appear.'

'June?'

'June Mockett. One of my hostesses.'

'Oh you have "hostesses", have you? I shouldn't have thought you'd have bothered for a few teenagers without much to spend.'

'You'd be surprised.'

'I daresay I would. I often am by what is called "the youth of today". You mean they can find money to throw about when they want to?'

'I don't know about throwing it about. They never seem short of a few bob.'

'How about Carver?'

Mr Swindleton looked like an insect impaled on a specimen board. His eyes went everywhere except to meet Carolus's eyes.

'Funny thing about Dutch,' he said at last. 'He always seemed able to find a quid or two and yet he never did a stroke of work. His parents were separated and didn't give him a bean. I never understood it.'

'This is the boy you don't know much about. You'd have to make enquiries before you could even say who were his associates. Perhaps it has all come back to you?'

'Don't be sarky, old man. You know how it is when someone asks you something. I just couldn't call it to mind for the moment. I remember Dutch now. Little peaky fellow...'

'Who was murdered,' ended Carolus bluntly.

'Yes. That's right. Or so they say. There doesn't seem to be much proof. From what I hear he might have had a smash on his bike.'

'Yes. So he might. As he was riding along naked with his bike in the garage.'

'You *are* a sarcastic bugger!' said Swindleton. 'Everything I say you have to be sarky about. What I meant was nobody seems able to account for his death. Unless you can?'

'Oh yes, I can. In several different ways and by a number of different people. But only one of them would be the right one. The trouble is finding that.'

'Must be. Yes,' said Swindleton who seemed scarcely to have heard what Carolus had said and looked jumpy and upset. 'Very difficult it must be. With all these teenagers you get nowadays.'

'You think that Dutch Carver was killed by his contemporaries?'

'I wish you wouldn't keep using words I can't understand. I never went to a university. I mean some of his mates. Teenagers, like him. You know the sort. Any of them might have done it.'

'Why?'

'That I can't say. Something to do with a girl perhaps. Or the length of his hair. They might have meant only to mug him and went too far. It might be anything. You've only got to read the papers.'

'Most of the crimes of violence among the young seem to be connected with drugs,' said Carolus.

'Don't you believe it, old man. Pot smokers are the quiet sort usually. Never do anyone any harm. All they want is a smoke and they're harmless as kittens.'

'Think so?'

Swindleton seemed to recollect himself.

'So I've been told, anyway,' he said.

'You don't know from personal experience?'

'Oh don't keep bringing that up again, old man. I've done my bird for that, so now you can surely let me alone. I didn't do anyone any harm.'

'It depends on what you call harm. *And* what you call "anyone".'

'Well, *anyone*. They'd have found the stuff if I hadn't sold them a little. That's what I told the Law. What d'you want to come down on me for? I said. If I hadn't sold them a little, someone else would have, I said, and probably much more. I was unlucky, that's what it was.'

Just then a good-looking girl, made up rather too noticeably, came into Swindleton's office.

' 'Lo darl,' Swindleton said.

The girl did not smile.

'I didn't know you were busy,' she answered with a glance at Carolus.

'Not really. Meet Mr Carolus Deene. This is June Mockett. How about pouring us a drink, ducks?'

The girl went to a cabinet obediently.

'What's yours Mr Deene?' she asked in a rich contralto voice. When Carolus briefly named a Scotch she said 'Would you like ice?' as though it was a matter of importance. Carolus said no, and there was a silence.

'Mr Deene's been asking about Dutch Carver,' Swindleton said.

'Poor Dutch!' said the girl feelingly.

'I believe he was quite a friend of yours,' Carolus said.

June smiled.

'I should scarcely say a friend,' she said. 'He was about ten years younger than me. I liked him all right.'

'But you knew him?'

'Oh, yes. I knew Dutch,' smiled June. 'We all did, didn't we Ron?'

'Mr Swindleton tells me he scarcely knew him at all,' put in Carolus quickly.

June tried to follow him.

'Perhaps not all that well,' she said. 'But we knew him. He came here.'

'On business?' Carolus asked.

'Mr Deene thinks I'm a pusher,' said Swindleton scornfully. 'He's heard all about me in Brighton and thinks every customer of this place only needs to be turned upside down for the pot to drop out of their pockets, don't you Mr Deene?'

'Yes,' said Carolus.

'There you are!' cried Swindleton indignantly. 'He knows it all. How about heroin? I suppose I traffic in that, too?'

'I shouldn't be surprised. I've got no actual proof of it yet.' Then Carolus added meaningly—'Dutch is dead, unfortunately.'

To Carolus's embarrassment Swindleton changed his tone of sarcastic indignation for sudden tearfulness.

'You see what he's doing to me, darl?' he enquired of June. 'It's not fair. It's not giving anyone a chance. You believe me, don't you, June?'

The girl looked at the wretched man and answered calmly—'Sometimes.'

'What d'you mean "sometimes"?' Swindleton shouted. 'You ungrateful bitch. Have I ever told you a lie?'

'Oh yes. Often. But you may not be lying about Dutch. I must say I never knew him to take the hard stuff.'

'Or handle it?' asked Carolus quietly.

'No,' said June. 'But of course I didn't know all that went on.'

'I'll say you didn't!' said Swindleton, then turning to Carolus he added—'Nothing went on. Nothing went on, I tell you. The kids came and had a dance in the evening. Didn't I learn my lesson when I was at Brighton? There was nothing more to it than that.'

'Nothing more except murder,' said Carolus. 'Aren't you forgetting that?'

'Murder? What's that to do with me? I suppose you're going to say next that I killed young Dutch?'

'Why should you have done?'

'That's what I want to know. There's got to be a reason before you throw accusations about, hasn't there?'

'Could be several reasons. Someone might have wanted to shut his mouth. Someone who had to hide something.'

'I suppose you're getting at me again. Well, you say what you like, Mr Deene. Say I murdered him and put his clothes in the furnace of the Sauna . . .'

'I certainly haven't said that,' said Carolus, showing interest. 'I didn't even know you had a Sauna bath.'

Swindleton seemed to grow almost hysterical. 'I haven't!' he shouted. 'I haven't! I was only showing you how ridiculous it is to connect me with Dutch's death.'

'Is there a Sauna bath here in Hartington?'

'Yes,' said June. 'It's called the Ringside. For men only.'

'D'you know it Mr Swindleton?'

'No. Yes. I don't know what I'm saying half the time, the way you carry on at me.'

'But do you?'

'Yes. I've been to it once or twice.' His voice rose. 'I've never seen the furnace. I don't even know that it's got a furnace. It may be heated by electricity. I wish you'd leave me alone. I've got work to do.'

'I'm sorry,' said Carolus, his manner changing to sudden amiability. 'I shouldn't have kept you talking all this time. We've all got our work to do, haven't we?' Then suddenly he threw out in a cool way which seemed to startle Swindleton more than ever—'When did you see Dutch last?'

But this misfired. As though with desperation Swindleton pulled himself together and said—'A week before he was missed, if you want to know. On the previous Sunday morning.'

'Where?' asked Carolus.

Swindleton did not bat an eyelid.

'In church,' he said. 'Singing a solo in the choir. He had a beautiful voice.'

June joined in to repeat her previous expression of sympathy. 'Poor Dutch!' she said. 'Poor little wretch.'

'You know he had two girl friends?' Carolus asked June.

'I only mentioned one,' reflected Swindleton, and turning to June, 'Jenny Rivers,' he explained.

'What about her friend?' asked Carolus.

'Which friend?'

'Big busty girl,' Carolus repeated from the description he had heard. 'Always got a grin on her face. Works at King's Supermarket. You'll nearly always find her on the vegetable counter.'

'He means Lotta,' said June.

'Oh, Lotta! Why didn't you say so? Yes, Dutch used to see quite a bit of Lotta. You might ask her if she knows anything.'

'What sort of thing?'

'What you're looking for. You've time to go round to King's Supermarket now. Just down the road. You'll nearly always...'

'Yes. On the vegetable counter. But there are still one or two things I want to ask you. For instance, did Dutch push for you?'

'I haven't the slightest idea what you mean,' claimed Swindleton. 'I told you he just came here for a dance or two.'

'Oh yes. That's what you said. But if he didn't, *who did*, Swindleton?'

'Why d'you keep on at me? I've told you that's all forgotten.'

'By the Law?'

'Well, it ought to be. I've got a clean sheet now. It's only when someone like you comes along and tries to mess it up I get jumpy. June here will tell you...'

'No she won't,' said June. 'You can both leave me out of this.'

'Well, she ought to tell you, after all I've done for her, the ungrateful bitch.'

'Actually,' June said with that infuriating tone that people adopt for the word. 'Actually I do think you're wasting your time, Carolus. This one hasn't the guts to kill a bluebottle, and I don't mean a policeman.'

'Of course he's wasting his time. Haven't I told him so?'

'You're not very convincing, either of you. Why not suggest another line of enquiry?'

'I'll do that,' said Swindleton. 'Try a woman called Bodmin.'

It seemed that June was surprised.

'Bodmin? D'you mean little Liz's mother?'

'Certainly I do. Didn't Dutch used to run round with the child?'

'Yes. But what...'

'You don't need to make a show of puzzling your brains—either of you. I know Mrs Bodmin.'

'I suppose it was her sent you to pester me?'

'No. As a matter of fact it wasn't. She suggested quite a different line of enquiry. But she knows you, I gather from that?'

'You gather something from everything. I've never seen the woman in my life. Not that I know of. I've only heard of her as being a fair old cow, letting her child run about the streets all day.'

Carolus stood up.

'There's only one more thing,' he said to Swindleton. 'Can you ride a motor-bike?'

'Can I? What's this in aid of? What d'you want to know for?' asked Swindleton rising to the question as Carolus thought he would. 'I haven't had a motor-bike for fifteen years or more.'

'I asked you if you could ride one?'

Swindleton flushed with fury said—'I don't bleeding know. I haven't tried—or not for donkey's years.'

'It's not a thing one forgets,' said Carolus coolly. 'Goodbye Mr Swindleton. Goodbye ... June is it?'

'June Mockett,' said the girl pronouncing the syllables with decision.

'Of course. That's it. Goodbye, June.'

Chapter Nine

A motor-bike came to a noisy halt in front of Carolus's house in Newminster and the rider pulled it up on its stand. Then two very strange-looking young men advanced to the front door.

Uncombed, and it would appear uncombable hair leaked down from under their crash-helmets which were ornamented with skull-and-crossbone designs crudely painted. It was impossible to distinguish their faces behind the eye-shields they wore.

Carolus heard the front door bell ring and a few minutes later Mrs Stick appeared in a state which might be called 'put out' 'upset' 'in a huff' or simply 'indignant'.

'I won't let them in!' she said. 'If you could see them, sir!'

'I can. I have,' said Carolus.

'It's not their dirty boots I mind, but they shouldn't be allowed in the house, not whatever you're trying to find out from them. They're not fit. I told them, I said, yes, Mr Deene's in, I said, but I don't suppose for a minute he'll see you, I said. They've got hair down their backs and I don't know what to think, whether they've come to stick a knife in you or whether they're what they call impersonators.'

'Surely you're used to the hair-styles of young men by this time, Mrs Stick?'

'Hair-styles I may be, but not looking like someone in a fair. How do we know we shan't have fleas in the furniture if they once get inside?'

'All right,' said Carolus. 'I'll take the responsibility. You needn't speak to them again.' He went out to the front door. 'I take it you're Phil White and Des Grayne? Come in. I was expecting you.'

'You were?' said Des as they came into the sitting-room. 'How come?'

They began to take off their outer protective clothing and dropped pieces of black macintosh into a corner of the room.

'Just a hunch, perhaps,' said Carolus. 'On the other hand you must have heard that I've seen Swindleton.'

They nodded rather solemnly.

'Yeh. We heard,' said Phil.

'What d'you want to tell me?'

There was great embarrassment on the faces of both of them, but finally the one called Des managed to get out what he wanted to say.

'If we was to come clean and tell you what we know, are you going to run to the Law and tell them?'

'Probably,' said Carolus. 'The police will have to be told if you've any material information.'

'What about pot? I mean if it had nothing to do with Dutch? What I mean is, if what we tell you helps to find out about Dutch, do you need to mention anything about Swindleton selling pot?'

'Look here,' said Carolus, cutting short these complicated hypotheses. 'I suggest you leave it to me. I shan't involve either of you in any enquiries except the identification of Dutch's murderer, or murderers. I don't know what you've got to tell me but I think

you'll be safe in my hands. That's about all I can say
till I know the rest.'

Des still wasn't satisfied.

'I mean you're not going to think because we grow
our hair a bit long and one thing and another we
have to be the ones who did Dutch, are you? See,
we've got something to tell you which looks bad for
us. You won't jump to any conclusions just because
some of our sort have got into trouble?'

'I certainly won't pre-judge the situation. Perhaps
you'd better go ahead?'

They exchanged glances and Carolus saw a nod
pass between them.

'It's like this,' began Des. ' 'Bout a week before
Dutch disappeared we were asked something by that
slimy bastard Swindleton. Nothing very much but ...
You tell him Phil.'

'He wanted us to give Dutch a good going over.
Said Dutch had let him down in some way. Wanted it
done properly to leave marks and that so as he wouldn't
think so much of himself with Jenny Rivers and Lotta.
Anyway that's what he said.'

'And you agreed?'

'Give us a chance,' said Des. 'You haven't heard it
all yet. He offered us fifty quid each.'

'Quite a lot of money,' said Carolus.

'I'll say. But it wasn't so much the money, only we
weren't feeling so good about Dutch either. See, he'd
... shall I tell him Phil?'

'Go ahead.'

'Well we'd been flogging pot for Swindleton and
making a bit on the side. I don't take the stuff myself.
Nor does Phil. It makes you spew, or it does me. But we
didn't see any harm in getting rid of a few packets for
Swindleton so long as he paid us for it. Then we found

he was telling us he hadn't received supplies and all he was doing was giving it to Dutch to get rid of, and Dutch seemed to have got all the customers. We were right needled about that so we told Swindleton we'd do him up properly and serve the poor bleeder right. Mind you, we wouldn't have done it if it wasn't for the pot.'

'I thought Dutch was a friend of yours?'

'Well, so he had been, I suppose in a way. Only fifty nicker each was good money for us, specially after what he'd been doing behind our backs.'

'At all events you agreed.'

'Not knowing what would come of it, mind you. Get that straight. We'd no idea anything else was going to happen to Dutch. All we was to do was give him a going over.'

'Go on.'

'There's a sort of a cellar under the Spook Club and a way out at the back into Ransome Street. But we didn't think of that. What Swindleton said was to get hold of Dutch when he came to the Club and take him downstairs. Then we were to give him a going over and when we'd done it to strip him off and tie him up. Then cut all his hair off.'

'What was the idea of that?'

'From what Swindleton said, it was to make Dutch look silly. I told you he'd told us Dutch had done him a dirty trick and he wanted to get his own back. He was going to take Jenny and Lotta down to the cellar to have a look at him like he was then. I didn't think much of that, but I'd heard of it being done before. Anyway we were getting fifty quid each so why should we worry?'

'Why indeed, if it did not strike you as rather a cowardly thing to do.'

'Well, I'm not saying it didn't afterwards, especially when we heard what had come of it. But we weren't to know. All we had to do was give Dutch a going over and tie him up.'

'And cut his hair. Some of you seem to attach quite a lot of importance to that. Regular little Samsons, aren't you? *And* strip the poor little wretch so that Swindleton could make him feel a fool in front of his girls.

'Yeh. I know. I've thought about it since. It wasn't what we ought to have done, I'll say that. But what I'm trying to say is that we didn't murder Dutch, or anything like it. Why we've come to you is that we heard you were investigating the whole thing and we didn't want to go to the Law. How were we to know what happened afterwards?'

'What *did* happen afterwards?'

'We don't know,' put in Phil, rather sulkily. 'We left him there in the cellar and that was the last we knew.'

'Was he all right then?'

'He'd been done up. We'd done the job pretty thoroughly. But he was all right—shouting at us to untie him and not leave him there. He never lost consciousness or anything like that. I'd say he could have walked out of that cellar and no one would have known anything about it except for his hair being cut and a couple of black eyes. I suppose everyone's been like that at one time or another. I know I have.'

'Did Swindleton give you your money?'

'Yes. He started some kind of talk about next day when he'd been to the bank but we said it had to be then or we should take Dutch away with us.'

'You didn't threaten to go to the police?'

'What you think we are? Bleeding grass-hoppers?'

Carolus stopped him there. His interest in the philology of criminal slang was aroused.

'What did you say?'

'Grass-hoppers. Shoppers,' said Des.

'So that's the origin of "grass". I thought it was "snake in the grass". Go on.'

'Soon as we said that, about taking Dutch away, he paid up.'

'And that's all you know?'

'Except that next day we asked Jenny and Lotta whether Swindleton had taken them down to the cellar and they said no.'

'Why do you think Swindleton wanted you in, then? Why couldn't he do it himself?'

'Too yellow. Ten to one Dutch would have given him a hiding if he'd tried.'

'Are you saying that a man as cowardly as that actually *murdered* Dutch?'

'Could have. When he was tied up. But I'm not saying that. I shouldn't be surprised if it wasn't someone else altogether.'

'What makes you think that?'

'The hundred nicker, for one thing. Swindleton's never been free with money. My idea, it was someone else's money he was giving us.'

'Anything else?'

'I've never known Swindleton want to get back on anyone, certainly not Dutch. Dutch has always been his blue-eyed bleeding boy. It was quite a laugh among the lads.'

'But who else could have wanted Dutch "done up" as you so expressively put it, except Swindleton?'

'Lots of people. His old man, for one. His old man was always on about Dutch living off him and not bringing home any bread. Or his old woman. Dutch

told that West Indian she lives with what he thought
of him once. The two had got it in for him.'

'What about Leng the organist? Or his friend
Skilly?'

'I wouldn't be surprised,' said Des. 'Though I can't
actually think of a reason why they might. Dutch
could be very saucy when he liked and one of them
might have taken offence. But I'll tell you who it could
have been, quite easily. One of the skinheads. Gil
Bodmin and those.'

'I should have thought they would do it themselves if they wanted to do it at all.'

'Not if they didn't want it blamed on them. Anyone
in this town would know that the first people anyone
would think of for beating up Dutch were the skinheads.'

'I've heard a lot about Dutch's brother Roger,' Carolus went on. 'Do you think he might have had some
sort of a grudge?'

'Quite likely. He's a smarmy sort of creep. But I
don't know of any reason.'

'You know,' Carolus said seriously. 'We seem to be
considering only the men. It occurs to me that one of
the women who knew Dutch might have got Swindleton to arrange it. Dutch's stepmother, as she would
like to be called, for instance?'

'That Farnham bitch, you mean? I don't put it past
her but where would the hundred nicker come from
in that case? Same with Liz Bodmin's mother. But it
could be some of the girls from the Spook Club. One
of them who was in the money from pushing, or
something.'

'It doesn't sound like a young girl, having a boy of
sixteen or seventeen beaten and tied up.'

'I don't know. What about his hair? It would take a

girl to think of that bit. Girls are always on to us to
have short haircuts.'

'That seems to leave only two probabilities. The
first is Swindleton himself. He struck me as a mean
and spiteful type. It could well be he felt a vicious
sort of vengefulness against Dutch and was willing to
pay you for what you did. From what you have admitted most of the money would come back to him,
anyway.'

'Yes, I suppose it could be Swindleton,' said Phil,
ignoring the last sentence. 'But we've told you we
don't think it was. What's your last probability?'

'You yourselves,' said Carolus without hesitation.
'Even if you didn't kill Dutch, all this story about
Swindleton having paid you to beat him up might be
so much balloney. I don't say it is, but it could be.'

'Then there's only one way to find out, isn't there?
Ask Swindleton himself. He's so shit-scared about
Dutch's being found dead that he'll tell you the truth
all right. He thinks he's going inside for life over
Dutch's death.'

'What about you, if that's so?'

'That's why we've come to you. I don't say we're
scared but I think you ought to know about it. Some-
body might think we'd overdone it. He was alive
enough when we left him.'

'What time was that?'

'Round about eleven, I should think.'

'And Dutch was dead an hour or two later, so the
doctors say.'

'Yes, but we didn't do him, did we?'

'The distinction seems to lie between "doing" someone, and "doing up someone". It's only a very small
word.'

'Christ, man! I thought you believed us. What we've

told you is the ——ing truth. All of it. Ask Swindleton.'

'Yes, I'm afraid I am faced with that unpleasant necessity. One interview with Swindleton's surely enough.'

'Ask that June Mockett, too. She lives near the Spook Club. If she doesn't know no one does.'

'Know who killed Dutch, do you mean?'

'That too, more than likely. Though she might try to say it was us.'

'Why?'

'She doesn't like us.'

'Nor do I, much. But that doesn't mean I should try to hang a murder on you.'

Des considered.

'I don't know how to take that,' he concluded. 'Sometimes you seem to be all right with us. At other times you might be the Law the way you go on.'

'Speaking about the Law, do you know Detective Sergeant Grimsby?'

Carolus had evidently startled them.

'Him?' said Des, panicking at the very name.

'You don't work with that bastard, do you?' asked Phil, seemingly horror-struck.

'I work with anyone who may help me to get at the truth. I see you both know him. How does that come about?'

'It was nothing really.'

'Only something to do with the bikes.'

'Detective Sergeant Grimsby is not a traffic cop,' Carolus pointed out.

'No. It wasn't much...'

'Pot?' asked Carolus.

'No. Nothing like that. Long time ago, it was. Coupla years at least.'

'Any charge?'

'There was going to be. Only my dad knew one of the coppers over at Newminster. He managed to get us off. It was only something to do with a girl.'

'Bit of a gang bang,' said Phil. 'Only she was quite willing. It turned out she'd tried it on before with some other fellows. That's why my dad managed to get Grimsby to drop it.'

'I don't think that's quite the story,' Carolus said.

'Well this girl's mother didn't want it to come out either. It wasn't as though we'd done the girl any harm. She's quite all right, I mean. Lives over at Boxley. I'm only telling you that because of Grimsby.'

'You mean because you think I should hear from Grimsby?'

'Something like that. Anyway we've told you now about Dutch.'

'You've told me something about him. I want a lot more than that.'

'You mean from us? We don't know any more.'

'Then you don't have to worry, do you?' said Carolus knowing from two anxious faces that there was a great deal more worrying to be done, whether or not there was any further information.

Chapter Ten

Carolus's second interview with Swindleton was very different from his first. He had no blind confidence in what the two boys had told him but he believed enough to feel pretty sure that Swindleton had bribed them to beat up Dutch Carver.

His expert manner of polite but ruthless bullying was excellently suited to Swindleton. And he took care that the *discothècaire* would not be on his own ground. He invited Swindleton to run out with him to the place where Dutch's body had been found. This Swindleton at first refused to do.

'Out there?' he asked nervously. 'Why out there? I don't know the place. I've never seen it.'

'Then it won't worry you, will it? I have to have another look, and as there are a few questions I want to ask you, I thought we could go together.'

'I'm not going!' said Swindleton.

'You *are* a nervous type,' said Carolus good-humouredly. 'It won't look at all well if you refuse, will it?'

'I'm not going, I tell you.'

'Then I shall have to put that in my report. It seems a pity, if you've got nothing to hide.'

'I haven't. But it seems so unnecessary. Creepy, too.'

'Let's get it over,' said Carolus. 'You won't even have to leave your seat in the car.'

Without any spoken consent Swindleton followed Carolus out to his car and they set off.

'Did you give those two friends of Dutch fifty quid each?' asked Carolus when they had pulled up a few miles out of Hartington and Carolus could turn to his passenger.

'Is that what they told you? Bloody little liars. I haven't got any fifty quids to chuck about.'

'Or was it for the pot business?' asked Carolus in the same steady tone of voice.

'Was *what* for the pot business? I never gave them anything.'

'Then what on earth made them beat up Dutch?'

'How do I know?' asked Swindleton. 'Kids are always scrapping. Might have been anything.'

'It might have been but it wasn't. It was a distinct and clearly worded bargain. They were to beat up Dutch, strip him off, cut his hair and tie him up, for which you would give them fifty quid apiece. It seems rather a large sum to pay for so simple a job, doesn't it?'

'I don't know what you're talking about.'

'No? Then I shall have to remind you. You gave them your reasons for wanting it done. Not very convincing reasons. They were connected with cannabis resin.'

'Leave that out!' said Swindleton. 'I've had enough trouble with that.'

'But don't you understand, Swindleton, that this isn't a case of selling kids a few ounces of pot. This is murder. A life sentence; and they're getting longer and longer.'

'Leave off, can't you?'

'It seems to me that if I were in your place I would admit the lesser things in the hope of not being charged with the greater. I don't suppose the whole scheme was entirely yours.'

Swindleton seemed to sway to and fro in the seat of the car. He was clearly in an agony of indecision.

'I don't know what to say.'

'Then I'll help you. You're a wretched creature but I don't want to see you given Life for something you haven't actually done. Who put up the money to have Dutch beaten up?'

Swindleton opened his mouth once or twice as though trying to speak. At last he came out with a surprising statement. 'I don't know!' he said.

Carolus repeated it incredulously.

'*You don't know?*'

'As God's my witness, I haven't the least idea.'

'But someone did?'

'Yes,' Swindleton whispered.

'But you don't know who it was. A hundred pounds landed in your lap from out of the sky?'

'No. It came through the post, in used treasury notes of £1.'

'Do you expect me to believe that?'

'No. That's why I couldn't tell you. Or anyone. No one would believe it. But it's true.'

'How did you know what to do with it?'

'I was telephoned.'

'I suppose you *don't know* who telephoned you?'

'No. I don't. It was a woman's voice. I couldn't recognize it. Working-class, it sounded like.'

'What exactly did it say?'

'I was just going to start out for the office one morning from where I live when the phone rang. "This is a friend," it said. Bloody nice sort of friend she turned out to be. I asked who was speaking but all she would say was "a friend".

'Then she said she wanted me to do a little job
for her. It would be to my own advantage she said.
I guessed what was coming then. She was going to put
the blacks on. "I know enough about your business to
be sure that you'll do what I want." I knew what that
meant. But I didn't say anything—just listened, trying
to make out who it was. "There's a boy round your
place named Carver, isn't there?" she asked. Again I
didn't answer but she knew without my saying anything. "I want him beaten up," she said, and added
"on Saturday night". I tried to tell her he wasn't a
bad boy whatever he'd done but she didn't seem interested. "Beaten up good and proper," she said. "It
needn't kill the little brute, just teach him a lesson."
You wouldn't have believed it was a woman at all the
way she went on.'

'Perhaps it wasn't,' said Carolus.

'The voice was, anyway. Then she gave more
details. She'd got it all worked out. It was to be done
in my cellar under the club. She gave the time and
everything. The boy was to be stripped off. I couldn't
believe my ears at that, from a woman, mind you.
Why? I asked her. "Never mind why. You listen," she
said, and told me how his hair was to be cut off and
burned with all his clothes. He was to be tied up and
left there. Then what? I asked her, because I didn't
like the idea of young Carver in that condition in my
cellar. "Leave the rest to us," she said. "Only close
up the club as soon as you can that night and then
keep away from it. Leave the yard gate open, and
the back door, and the door down to the cellar. That's
all." I asked her how I was going to get anyone to
rough-house Carver and she told me about the hundred nicker. "Only mind it all goes on the job," she
said. "Don't try nibbling or you'll have had it.

Hand it over to those who do it—all the lot. You'll get it through the post the day after tomorrow. Everything understood?"

'I understood all right but it made me feel ill thinking about it. I never have liked violence and I could feel this was a wicked cruel bitch talking. Imagine a woman wanting that done! And the boy not seventeen!'

Carolus said nothing but drove on.

'It's a very strange story,' he said. 'But she'd picked the right man. You carried it out to the letter.'

'I didn't want to. I felt sick when I heard the poor little blighter's screams coming up from the cellar. But what could I do? You hear a voice coming like that from nowhere on the telephone and it turns you up, I can tell you. I had to do what she said and I handed over every penny of the money.'

Swindleton sounded almost proud of that.

'Did you see the two boys Phil and Des after they'd been to work on Dutch?'

Swindleton looked slyly at Carolus, perhaps wondering that he knew who had done the job for him.

'Yes. I paid them off! Gave them every ...'

'You've already said that. And did you leave the club soon after they did?'

'Yes.'

'Without going down to the cellar?'

Swindleton looked desperate. 'Yes! Yes! Of course. I couldn't go down there after what I'd heard.'

'Then what?' asked Carolus.

He had reached exactly the place where Stick had found the body. He watched Swindleton closely but could see no trace of recognition in his face. Either he was a clever actor or he had not been here before.

'Then what? As soon as I'd had my breakfast next

morning I went round to the club. Gate into the yard closed, back door unlocked, cellar door unlocked and no sign of Carver. I thought I might find him upstairs on one of the settees, sleeping it off, poor little sod. But he was nowhere. Gone. Taken away. Then, in a couple of days I read about their finding his body, and saw the whole thing.'

'Meanwhile you did not think of reporting what had happened to the police?'

Carolus could see the man stiffen in his seat. The word police had gone home like a shot.

'No,' he said. 'I didn't. If you knew the police like I do you wouldn't be so keen to go running to them for every little thing.'

'But this wasn't a little thing, Swindleton, it was murder. With a bloody big M.'

'I know that now, or I suppose I do, but how was I to know at the time? I thought it was like the woman said, just to beat him up and humiliate him.'

'And now that you do know?'

'I suppose it was all a plot. All worked out to bring me into it.'

'Yes. But why? Why should anyone go to that trouble, or spend that money, simply to involve you?'

'I don't know. I really don't.'

'Do you recognize this place?'

For the first time Swindleton looked about him. Carolus was sure now that he wasn't acting.

'This place? You mean ... this is where they found him?'

'Just here.'

'Never seen it before in my life. Never been along this road unless it was to run straight in to Newminster.'

'Good. Now about the voice on the telephone. Working-class you said?'

'Yes. Well you know what I mean.'

'I do. Did it sound put on?'

'Not a bit. Quite natural.'

'And you still don't recognize it?'

'No. I've thought and thought...'

'Let's see what voices you know. Have you heard Carver's mother speaking?'

'Flo, you mean? It wasn't her. I know her voice. Trying to be ritzy, isn't it? No, it wasn't her.'

'What about Mrs Farnham?'

'I know that, too. Couldn't mistake it.'

'What about the girls? What about June, for instance?'

'She was about all the time.'

'In the room?'

'Well, not actually in the room. But round the club somewhere. It couldn't have been her.'

'Or any of the younger girls?'

'No. I'd have known them.'

'Then Mrs Bodmin?'

'I did just wonder once whether it could have been her. But she was very fond of Dutch. She wouldn't have done all that to him.'

'Of course you may never have heard the voice before. It might have been someone from a distance brought in.'

'I suppose so. And yet there did seem something familiar about it.'

'Anyway, it worked. You did what you were told and...'

'What else could I do? You tell me that. I couldn't have done anything else.'

'And as a result,' Carolus went on inexorably. 'Young Carver was murdered.'

'But I didn't mean him to be. Surely you believe that? I'd no idea they were up to anything like that.'

'They?'

'Whoever did it.'

'Have you any suggestion?'

'I suppose it could have been the lads I put on to it. They're quite capable of taking the money and doing him too.'

'But you say you didn't go down to the cellar after they'd finished?'

'I've told you I didn't. I'm sensitive to that sort of thing. I wouldn't have slept that night if I'd seen Dutch like he was.'

'But I suppose you slept like a top knowing he was tied up?'

'Of course I didn't. I didn't sleep a wink the whole night. But it would have been worse if I'd seen him.'

'You don't seriously believe it was Des and Phil who killed him?'

'I don't know. If you'd heard the way he was screaming you might have.'

'Anyone else on your list of suspects?'

'It could have been the other boys, the skinheads.'

'What makes you think that?'

'They're dead against the greasers, like Dutch.'

'But to kill?'

'It seems funny that he was carried out on the back of a motor-bike. They're the ones that use motor-bikes all the time.'

'What happened to Dutch's clothes?'

'I burned them, like the woman said.'

'Where?'

'In the furnace in the cellar.'

'Thoroughly?'

'I'll say. I didn't want any bits of his clobber found.'

'It was all there?'

'As far as I could see, yes. In a corner of the cellar.'

'So how would you suppose he was taken away on the pillion of a motor-bike in public?'

'They might have had other clothes, mightn't they?'

'Yes. Who else do you suspect?'

'It seems a bit funny to say so but both the boy's parents would have been glad to be rid of him. Or that's the impression I got.'

'Yes. You've named everyone but yourself.'

'Me?' shouted Swindleton. 'You must be out of your mind. Me kill Dutch? He was my friend, I tell you. I wouldn't have...'

'Touched a hair of his head? You arranged for it to be cut off. His hair, I mean.'

'That was just part of what I thought was a scheme. Almost a joke. Can't you understand that? If I had known how it was to turn out I wouldn't have...'

'Wouldn't have what?'

'Well, got into it at all.'

'You say you couldn't help it. You were forced to do what you did.'

'You twist everything round. You don't know what it is to have done a bit of bird and have the Law watching you every minute of the day. I just haven't the strength to say no when I'm being threatened. Can't you understand that?'

'I suppose so,' said Carolus. 'It depends on how you're made.'

Carolus drove on in silence for a while then said—'You know Swindleton, curiously enough I believe most of what you've said today. That is up to the point where Phil and Des left their friend tied up in the cellar. After that about what happened I have an open mind.'

'But surely you must have come to some conclusions from what I've told you?'

'No. "Conclusions" is altogether the wrong word. I'm still fumbling about among guesses. I hoped what you told me would—I don't say decide anything—but at least enable me to cross out a few things that had been possibilities. Narrowed down the pursuit, that is. I thought I might be able to say "It wasn't *that*. And it certainly wasn't *that*." But it's done nothing of the sort. All the possibilities are still there—as large as life. I have to go much farther before I can begin to decide.'

'And you mean to do so. Why in hell do you want to bother yourself? The boy wasn't worth it.'

'The boy? What's the boy to do with it? It's murder I'm interested in, not some scrubby little wretch of whom many people would say he deserved it.'

'You mean you want to get someone into the nick for fifteen years?'

'Not that exactly, either. I want to wipe the slate clean. I've been given this peculiar faculty of getting at the truth in a case like this and I daren't fail to use it. I mean that. I daren't turn my back on a problem. I don't suppose you can understand that, Swindleton.'

'In a way perhaps I do. You mean it sort of comes natural to you? You do it just the same now as when there was the death penalty?'

'That,' said Carolus, 'made no difference at all. And now we'll drive back and I'll leave you at your infamous club.'

He did that.

Chapter Eleven

Carolus phoned Grimsby to make an appointment.

'At the station?' suggested Grimsby.

'No. I don't think your Station Sergeant cares for me much. Why don't you come to my house?'

'Because I'm sure your housekeeper doesn't care for me *at all*,' retorted Grimsby. 'And that's putting it mildly. But I'll come. Be round in about fifteen minutes.'

When they had both relaxed over a drink Carolus asked, 'Who's in charge over at Hartington?'

'Uniformed branch, you mean? Inspector Goad.'

'Approachable, would you say?'

'He's all right. Why?'

'I want to ask for something which he's pretty well bound to turn down, though he might come round to it later without telling me.'

'Oh come on, Carolus. Drop the mystery.'

'I want him to have a watch kept on the little girl, Liz Bodmin.'

This seemed to astound Grimsby. He remained quite silent then said—'I thought she was out of it.'

Carolus went on as though he hadn't heard.

'Not too obvious a watch but a pretty careful one. The child may be in danger.'

'In *danger*?'

'Yes. I may be wrong but I think your people ought to know.'

'Why can't you give the details? It's rather a lot to expect of them to keep a watch on a child on your say-so, without giving any sort of reason.'

'I know it is. That's why I asked you about Goad.'

Grimsby made a decision.

'It'll be sticking my neck out but I'll do what I can. We'll go over and see Goad together.'

'Now?' suggested Carolus.

'Well if it's all that dangerous I suppose the sooner the better.'

It was late when they reached Hartington and at the police station they were told by a cheery and over-informative duty officer that Inspector Goad had gone home.

'But you'll find him at his house in Newminster Road. Number 16 it is. He's probably just got down to his evening paper.'

'Thanks,' said Grimsby.

'Reads that every night regularly,' said the informative one. 'Hasn't time to read a morning paper he says. We've been pretty busy lately.'

'Have you?'

'Yes. Small stuff. Lots of shoplifting we get round here.'

'Break-ins?' asked Grimsby politely.

'Not extra. A few elevenses.'

Carolus asked what the term implied.

'Round about eleven o'clock in the morning when housewives are out shopping we get one or two of them going round pretending they're collecting or selling vacuum cleaners and that. They just try the door or look for a back window then see what there is about. You'd be surprised what they pick up. One woman yelled the place down because they'd taken her husband's camera which had a film in it—pictures of their baby. You get all sorts,' he added as a philosophical end-piece.

'Many car thefts?'

'Very few, thank God. They're a bloody nuisance. We had one last night, funnily enough, or so the owner said. Little chap named Skilly. He rang up this morning to say he'd found it, just as though it was a lost pet.'

'Perhaps it was,' said Grimsby. 'Some owners fuss over their cars as though they were alive. We must be getting on, though. We've got to see the Inspector.'

That was an unfortunate remark because it set off a mass of repetition from the desk officer, how to find the house, the fact that Goad was a widower and would be on his own and so on. But at last they got away and found number 16 Newminster Road which turned out to be a tidy bungalow with a feature which always annoyed Carolus, a winding path up to the front door to make it appear as though the distance from the front gate was greater.

Inspector Goad, a grey-haired man of fifty-odd was alert-looking and spoke quickly. He invited them into the room where he had been sitting in a deep armchair with a tankard beside him. The evening paper, as the duty officer had predicted, lay beside his chair.

'I can only offer you beer,' said Goad. Grimsby accepted at once and Carolus did so too.

'Now what can I do for you, gentlemen?' asked Goad.

'Mr Deene has something to ask you,' said Grimsby, then added—'Between ourselves I may say that Mr

Deene has been of considerable help to me in that case over in my manor.'

'The dead boy found in a ditch, you mean?'

'Yes.'

Goad pulled at his pipe but said nothing for a moment.

'Well, Mr Deene?' he asked at last.

'This is very difficult,' Carolus admitted. 'First of all I must admit, Inspector, that I'm a private individual. I haven't even got the pretence of a status in the case which an investigator employed by the family might have.'

'That's good,' interjected Goad. 'At least you admit it. You mean you're just inquisitive?'

'That's it,' said Carolus. 'Just inquisitive.'

'Mr Deene has some reputation as a criminologist,' put in Grimsby.

'I know that,' said Goad sharply. 'I can read, you know. I've had a lot of entertainment out of reading detective novels, Mr Deene, from Sherlock Holmes onwards.'

'Sherlock Holmes!' said Grimsby with the contempt of the present generation. 'Conan Doyle wrote of the police as though they were a lot of stupid illiterates!'

'Perhaps they were in those days,' said Inspector Goad. 'And one or two of them aren't much better today.'

Grimsby accepted the reproof.

'Whereas,' went on Goad, 'I've never met a private investigator. Certainly not one who admits that it is no more than a hobby.'

'Hobbies grow,' said Carolus. 'They start small and gradually take over the whole mind.'

'You specialize in murder?'

'I *only* investigate murder.'

'I should have thought that was something of a disability,' said Goad. 'It's the variety of our work which gives us insight. And you need insight to understand a murderer.'

Carolus admitted it.

'I gather yours is a more scholarly approach than ours. You wrote a book called *Who Killed William Rufus?* didn't you?'

'Many years ago I did.'

'Interesting,' said Goad. 'Now what have you come to see me about?'

'You'll think it's what is called a liberty,' said Carolus. 'I've come to ask you to have a special watch kept on a little girl in Hartington.'

'I suppose you don't want to explain?'

'As far as I can, yes. I believe the child may be in danger. What I can't tell you, because I really don't know with any certainty, is the identity of the person from whom she may be in danger.'

'That's *very* Holmes,' said Goad. 'With a touch of the patronizing manner of Lord Peter Wimsey. You "don't know with any certainty". No. But you've got a pretty good idea, haven't you Mr Deene?'

'I must admit I have made some wild guesses.'

'Oh come. I'm not going to press you. You've got your public to consider, haven't you? Revelation right at the end while the police are gasping with astonishment! I know. I know. But you shall have what you want because you don't come to me with a tale of "having reason to know that the child may be kidnapped at any minute".'

'If I had done that it would have been "murdered" not "kidnapped",' said Carolus.

'Oh it would? And you really think that?'

'I think if it happened at all it would be murder.'

Goad was thoughtful.

'How old is the child?'

'About twelve.'

'Moors stuff, eh?'

'In a way, perhaps.'

Goad took up the phone. Carolus was amused to see that he had to dial the Station number, having no private line.

'Is WPO Major there?' he asked, and when he was connected—'Oh, Barbara. Could you come round for a few moments?'

The answer was audible to them all.

'Rather!' said Barbara cheerily. 'I'll hop on the bike and come round.'

She was, as old-fashioned story-tellers say, as good as her word. A motor-bike roared up to the gate and a hefty female figure came up to the front door in three paces, ignoring the squiggles of the path.

'Yes, Chief?' the two heard her say, doubtless wringing Goad's hand.

Carolus prepared for his introduction. WPO Major gave her hearty handshake to each in turn. Then with her mighty legs far apart she prepared to listen to Goad.

'What's the trouble?' she asked.

'We want you to keep an eye on a child,' said Goad and Carolus was grateful for the tact of that 'we'.

'What sort of child?'

Carolus took it up.

'A little schoolgirl named Liz Bodmin. Her mother's at work all day and hasn't much time for the child.'

'Why can't she look after herself? Case of dirty old men?'

'The child is very young for her age,' began Carolus patiently.

'Arrested development?' asked the WPO.

'You might call it that, though she's bright enough in some ways. I found her quite a charming little girl.'

'Oh, you did?' said WPO Major and looked at Carolus as though she thought he might be one of the dirty old men she suspected. 'Have you been on to the Headmistress, Chief? She should be able to take precautions,' and she glanced again at Carolus.

'Not yet,' said Goad. 'We've only just been given the information. I will do so today.'

'Good-o.'

'But the school can only be responsible in school hours. We need more than that. This might be a case of murder.'

'Murder, by jove!' exclaimed the WPO, as though this were a particularly juicy possibility.

'No,' corrected Carolus, who found the big woman's manner a trifle hard to take. 'By someone locally.'

'We are not in a position to state anything more than that,' said Goad. 'Will you take it on, Barbara?'

'You can bet your bottom dollar I will. Dirty old men are just my tea. I can handle them half-a-dozen at a time.'

'Good. But I don't want the child to know she's watched.'

'I shan't be noticed,' promised Barbara. 'I can be quiet as a lamb when I need to be.'

'I will roar you as gently as any sucking dove,' said Grimsby who had evidently been studying *A Midsummer Night's Dream*.

'Shut up, Grimsby,' said Barbara.

'I must tell you,' said Goad seriously, 'that this is a case in which some considerable danger is involved. To the child, I mean.'

Barbara seemed sobered. 'Let's have all the gen, Chief,' she said.

'Mr Deene will give you what information he can.' This Carolus did and was not surprised to find that WPO Major, under her bluff exterior, had a keen and efficient mind, and became acquainted with all the details most intelligently.

'Right-o,' she said closing her notebook with a snap. 'Let me get at him, whoever he is.'

'May not be a him,' warned Goad.

'True. But it's ten to one,' said Barbara. 'Anyhow you can depend on me, Chief. Just my job.'

'I am going round to see the mother this evening,' said Carolus.

'You can hop up on my pillion,' offered Barbara, 'and we can see her together.'

'I think I should see her alone first,' said Carolus, smiling his gratitude for the offer.

'Okey-doke. I'll nip round and case the house later. Right. So are we all set? I'll report tomorrow Chief.'

Her motor-bike made a loud noise as she started it. She rode off.

'I shouldn't like to be what she calls a dirty old man if your WPO got her hands on him,' said Grimsby. 'But she's good at her job,' he admitted.

When Goad had poured out some more beer he turned unexpectedly to Carolus.

'I've just remembered where I've seen you before Mr Deene,' he said.

'Really. Where?'

'Here in Hartington, unless I'm mistaken.'

'Quite likely. I've been over here a lot lately.'

'Oh, you have? The dead boy came from here, of course.' Then he added, looking keenly at Carolus, 'This was last night.'

'Last night? I must have been motoring home.'

'No. You were on foot.'

'On *foot*? I'm never on foot if I can help it!'

Goad did not smile responsively.

'You were last night,' he said.

'What time would it have been?'

'Latish. I was just coming home from a friend's house where we'd been playing Bridge. Could have been two o'clock. Is that right?'

Carolus grinned.

'I see you know all my secrets,' he said.

Grimsby seemed rather offended.

'You never told me you were over here last night,' he said.

'There was no need to. I've always been a bit of a noctambule.'

'Night-walker's right,' said Goad. 'Where was your car, Mr Deene?' It was not a question as a policeman asks questions, but it sounded as though Goad wanted an answer.

'In the yard of the Royal Oak,' said Carolus. 'I was just going to pick it up. It's open all night. I'd been in the bar earlier.'

Goad, having been answered, was all smiles.

'Yes, I thought it was you,' he said. 'I knew as soon as you came in that I'd seen you before, but it took me a few minutes to remember when and where.'

'It's a small world,' said Grimsby sarcastically. 'No wonder I couldn't get you on the phone last night, Carolus. But your housekeeper didn't say you'd gone to Hartington.'

'No. Why should she? I warned you that Mrs Stick finds it very hard to distinguish between policemen and criminals. It's not her fault. I have friends among both.'

But as though to compensate Grimsby for his lack of co-operative friendliness, Carolus suggested, when they had left Goad, that the two of them should go and see Mrs Bodmin together, and this they did.

Chapter Twelve

At 47 Docker Street Carolus obtained a certain insight
into the way the police were received into a home
like this. The tall pale Mrs Bodmin appeared pleased
to see Carolus, though she was incapable of being
effusive, but when Carolus introduced Detective Sergeant Grimsby her manner changed at once.

'What do you want to see *me* for?' she asked, more
of Grimsby than of Carolus.

'Is Liz in?' asked Carolus ignoring the question.

'She's just run out for something. She'll be home in
a few minutes.'

'That's rather what I wanted to see you about, Mrs
Bodmin,' said Carolus.

'Why? What's she been up to?'

It was clear that Mrs Bodmin was determined to
treat this as 'a visit from the police' and nothing else.

'It's nothing that she has done,' went on Carolus.
'It's something that we're afraid may happen to her.'

If Mrs Bodmin had been a horse one would have
said that she tossed her mane. As it was one must
admit that her movement was not unlike that.

'Don't you worry about Liz,' she said. 'She can take
care of herself. She doesn't need any police running

round after her. She's *quite* all right on her own, thank you very much, and if she wasn't I shouldn't let her go out as I do.'

'But Mrs Bodmin,' went on Carolus reasonably, realizing that it was a mistake to have brought Grimsby however discreetly he was behaving. 'You won't mind if I tell you something which we find rather worrying?'

'If it's about Liz I don't want to hear it. Liz is as able to look after herself as you or me. Better, very likely. So it's no good telling me different and bringing a policeman round to frighten me into thinking it, with all the neighbours watching who comes in or out and knowing him very likely whether he's in plain clothes or not.'

'It's quite dark outside,' said Carolus mildly.

'Not dark enough for them, it isn't; they've got eyes everywhere and know more about your business than what you know yourself.'

She paused to take breath and Carolus seized the advantage.

'I know you have to work hard and be away from home a great deal, Mrs Bodmin; that's why I'm worried about Liz.'

'There's no call to be, I can tell you that and ...'

But Carolus, once in the saddle rode on. 'I have to tell you that there is very real danger for your little daughter. I know you wouldn't like anything to happen to her.'

'Nothing is going to happen to her,' said Mrs Bodmin but with less assurance than before.

'Let's hope not. But there's a danger of it. I have been trying to find out about young Kenneth Carver's death, as you know ...'

'That's different. There was plenty of them wanted

him out of the way. Who's going to hurt a child of eleven?'

'I thought she was twelve.'

'So she may be but I can't remember everything. I say, who's going to hurt a child like that?'

'Will you believe me when I tell you that there is someone who wants to do so? Someone who would like to see her dead?'

Mrs Bodmin's jaw dropped and she was silent for a whole half minute.

'You mean, same as Dutch?' she asked with something like a gasp.

'Not necessarily the same person, or even for the same reason, but the result could be the same.'

'Oh my God!' said Mrs Bodmin, for the first time being visibly startled.

Carolus was about to go on when the woman rose and hurried to the street door.

'Liz!' she shouted. 'Come here when I tell you! Liz!' She spoke to someone invisible. 'Have you seen Liz, Mrs Nustle?' she demanded in a somewhat peremptory voice.

'She was round here about half an hour ago,' replied the invisible person. 'I should think she's gone down to Castles's. That's where she usually goes.'

'She isn't with your Freda, is she?'

'No. Freda's been home half an hour or more, doing her homework. It's a pity your Liz hasn't got young Dutch to look after her any more. You never know with kiddies nowadays. Look what you read in the paper! It doesn't bear thinking about. Here, who's that coming up the road? Isn't that your Liz? She's not hurrying, is she?'

Mrs Bodmin let out a yell like a hyena.

'Liz!' she shouted. 'Come here at once, will you?

I'll smack your bottom, you see if I don't! Making me worry like that! There's a policeman after you and was going to take you away in a minute if you didn't come. Wherever have you been?'

Liz entered, seeming quite calm.

'I got your fags mum. Here's the change.'

'You go straight up to bed, you naughty girl, you. Frightening me like that. And don't you ever dare to go out alone, do you hear? Up you go and don't let me hear another sound.' She turned to Carolus and Grimsby. 'You see what I have to put up with? It's enough to upset anyone, with you telling me she's going to be murdered same as Dutch. I don't know where to turn.'

Grimsby spoke for the first time.

'It's all right, Mrs Bodmin. The Inspector's going to have the little girl watched as far as he can.'

'Watched?' It was clear there could only be one meaning for the word in the present circumstances. 'Watched what for?'

'I should have said "watched over". One of our women police officers is going to help protect Liz.'

'Women police officer? Lot of use she'll be if they mean to murder the child. She'll be no more use than Liz herself.'

Carolus wanted to say 'you should see her!' but resisted the temptation, and only said that WPO Major was quite capable of looking after Liz.

'If you say so,' said Mrs Bodmin.

'Though we hope you will watch over her yourself, when you are home from work. Nobody can be there all the time.'

'Oh yes, I will. And so will Mrs Nustle next door. Her little girl Freda's very good with Liz and she'll keep an eye open if anything happens. Liz is in and

out of Nustles's half the time when I'm not here so
she ought to be all right. I hope this woman policeman
of yours won't be wearing uniform when she comes
here? It gives anyone a bad name in the district.'
'Oh no. She'll be very careful of that,' promised
Grimsby. 'Anyhow she's coming to see you first, so
you can tell her.'
Mrs Bodmin did her best to express gratitude to
Grimsby, though always with the reserve that any
contact with the police seemed to call forth. Then
Grimsby, at a signal from Carolus, took his leave.
'Mrs Bodmin,' said Carolus confidentially when
they were alone together. 'I want to ask you some-
thing.'
'I suppose you can,' said Mrs Bodmin, not very
graciously.
'When I was here before, I gathered from Liz herself
that she had a secret shared with Kenneth Carver.
When I mentioned this, you thought I was implying
that the boy had interfered with Liz or something of
the sort.'
'And I told you it was nonsense,' said Mrs Bodmin.
'Yes. If I had suggested that, I quite believe that it
would have been. But they had a secret together all
the same. I'm pretty sure of that now.'
'What sort of secret?'
Carolus hesitated.
'I think,' he said, 'though I'm not sure, that it
concerned someone else.'
This took a moment to be fully understood.
'You mean, you think some other bastard had inter-
fered with my little girl?'
'It's just possible.'
'I don't believe it. Not for a minute, I don't. Liz
tells me everything.'

'D'you think so, Mrs Bodmin?'

The same expression came over her face as had been aroused when Carolus had told her that someone wanted to see Liz dead.

'Well, I've always thought so. D'you mean to say something may have happened that I don't know about?'

'I know you have to work very hard...'

'Never mind the work. What you're saying is that someone got hold of Liz and Dutch knew about it but I didn't?'

'I'm afraid it could be that.'

Instead of flaring up as she was accustomed to do, Mrs Bodmin seemed to think this over.

'How long ago do you think it might have been?' she asked.

'It's impossible to say. I'm not even sure that it happened.'

'No, but you must be pretty certain or you wouldn't have mentioned it at all. If it is true and I could get hold of the man who did it I'd kill him. Straight I would. I don't say I've been the best mother in the world to Liz, having to go to work and that, but this is something that doesn't bear thinking about. It's horrible. Horrible.'

'I'm going to ask you to help bring it home to whoever's guilty. Do you think you can get Liz to tell you the truth about it now?'

To Carolus's great embarrassment there were tears in Mrs Bodmin's eyes.

'I think so, I'll try,' she blurted out.

'You won't do it by threatening her,' Carolus said. 'And I'm afraid she won't tell you while she thinks that Dutch will be coming back. She promised him to keep the secret, you see. He gave her presents but that is not the important thing. She loved Dutch. It's good to know that one human being at least loved that unfortunate boy. So it will take a lot of tact and care to get it out of her. You're the only person who can do it.'

Some of the spirit returned to Mrs Bodmin.

'What about the policewoman?' she asked.

'Liz isn't even to know that she is a policewoman or looking after her. Anyhow she could never get the secret from Liz. But I'm sure you can.'

'That's more than I am. Liz is a funny child; if she makes up her mind about something wild horses wouldn't change her. If she promised Dutch she wouldn't tell I don't know how I'm ever going to find out. I'll try, of course. But don't blame me if she decides to shut up like an oyster. Then we shall never know.'

'Unless...' said Carolus.

'Unless what?'

'It takes two to keep a secret. Dutch's dead, but do you think he could have told anyone else his side of it?'

'I should have thought if he told anyone it would have been me. Or one of the lads he went about with.'

'Phil and Des, you mean? I'm afraid not. I've talked to them and I'm pretty sure they know nothing.'

'It certainly wasn't Connie Farnham. That's a sure thing. He wouldn't have opened his mouth to her even to tell her her house was on fire. Tell you what, though. There is someone he used to see. That West Indian who's living with Flo Carver. I won't call her Dutch's mother because she behaved no more like a mother to him than the man in the moon. But Dutch might have said something to that Justus Delafont as he calls himself.'

'What on earth had those two in common?'

'Pot,' replied Mrs Bodmin, bringing out the word as though she was firing it from a pea-shooter. 'He used to take him his pot which he got from Swindleton. I don't say they ever talked much together but it might be worth a try.'

'Yes, indeed.'

'Tomorrow's Sunday,' remembered Mrs Bodmin. 'If you were to go round in the morning you'd find him at home. He never goes to the Wheatsheaf on Sunday morning same as all the others because there was some Trouble there. And she goes to church to show off. So you'd get a chance to speak to him.'

'Thanks. I will. And you will remember all we've agreed about Liz, won't you?'

'I shall. It's given me a shock, Mr Deene, which I shan't get over in a hurry. But you may depend on me doing what I can.'

So next morning after telling Mrs Stick that he wouldn't be home to lunch, Carolus drove up to the house in which he had interviewed Flo Carver, or Estelle Delafont as she preferred to be called, and hoped he could reach the front door before the friendly neighbour spotted him. But the hope was vain.

'She's gone to church,' said the neighbour. 'St Thomas's. She won't be back yet awhile because Reverend Wilkinson's preaching this morning and he always goes on for hours, till people's dinners are all spoilt. He's lost a lot of the congregation that way and I must say I can't blame them. I go to Early Service at All Saints and have it over with. Did you want to see her again?'

'Thank you. Don't trouble. I wanted to have a word with Mr Delafont if he's in.'

'Oh he's in all right. He's out the back mowing the lawn, what there is of it. It's no good ringing because he can't hear you. Wait till I tell him.' She raised her voice, facing towards the back of the house. 'Mr Delafont!' she screamed. 'Someone to see you! It's all right. He's heard. He'll be out in a minute.'

And he was, a tall surly-looking West Indian going bald on the top of his head.

'Yes?' he said to Carolus.

'Good-morning, Mr Delafont,' Carolus tried to sound breezy. 'Can you spare me a few minutes?'

'What is it you want?'

Carolus saw that it was going to be hard going and would not be rendered easier by the fact that the kindly neighbour continued to lean out of her window as though, having brought the two men together, she had a right to join in their conversation.

'Perhaps if I could come inside for a moment?' suggested Carolus.

'I don't see what you want to come inside for,' said Mr Delafont, but after glancing round he moved aside invitingly. 'That woman next door wants to know everything,' he said as if to explain his invitation. 'Now what is it you want?'

There was nothing for it but to plunge right in.

'You knew the boy known as Dutch Carver, I believe?'

'Certainly I did. His mother's my friend.'

A nice way of putting it, thought Carolus.

'I'm trying to discover who killed him,' he said.

Mr Delafont turned hostile.

'Oh you are, are you? Well don't come to me, because I didn't.'

'I wasn't suggesting such a thing. But Dutch had some secret information . . .'

This was worse.

'Maybe he had and maybe he hadn't. He never told me about any secret information so it's no good asking me.'

'I thought perhaps as you knew the boy you might like to help discover who murdered him,' said Carolus reproachfully.

'All I know is I didn't.'

'Did he ever mention the little girl Liz Bodmin to you?'

'That I can't remember,' said Mr Delafont too readily.

'Or any of the skinheads? Gil Bodmin, the little girl's cousin? Or a boy they called Trimmer?'

'You can go on giving me names all day and all night and I can't remember them. So what's the good of talking?'

It was probably of no use, Carolus agreed, but he persisted.

'What about the ones with hair like his, Des and Phil? Do either of their names ring a bell?'

A broad grin suddenly stretched across Mr Delafont's face.

'Ring it!' he said. 'Go on, man! Ring it for all you're worth and see if that makes any difference. I tell you I don't know anything about it.'

'But you know a girl called June?'

Delafont's face was suddenly clouded with fury.

'Who says I know any girl? Someone's been telling you a lot of lies, mister. I don't know any girl, June, July or September. And now I'll thank you to get going before Mrs Delafont comes back and finds you here!'

Carolus went.

Chapter Thirteen

As he was climbing into his car a cheery voice called from the pavement.

'Hullo, there! I've been looking for you. I'm Roger Carver!'

Carolus saw a healthy-looking young man of twenty-one or so, conventionally dressed and with hair which represented a compromise between the long tresses of the greasers and the Cromwellian polls of the skinheads. He was smiling and offering a broad hand which Carolus took.

'You're investigating the death of my young brother,' he said. 'I may be able to tell you something.'

Carolus showed no great enthusiasm. He had a distrust, formed through many past experiences, of those who volunteer information so readily. But he knew better than to refuse it.

'I was just going to have a drink at the Wheatsheaf,' Carolus said. 'Like to come along?'

'Right,' said Roger and climbed into Carolus's car.

'You know Grimsby, the CID man?' asked Roger.

A curious kind of name-dropping, Carolus thought, but said, 'Yes.'

'I haven't told him what I know,' said Roger, perhaps thinking that Carolus would applaud this.

'Why not?'

'I'm not all that mad on the Law. I intended to keep it for you.'

'You should have reported anything you know to Grimsby. He's in charge of the case. I'm just an inquisitive amateur.'

'I know. That's why I preferred to tell you.'

They drew up at the Wheatsheaf and found the bar crowded with that peculiar collection which meets in English pubs before lunch on Sunday, the soiled flannels and untidy blazers of the more pretentious gentry who have worn city suits all the week, contrasting with the machine-tailored suits of those who have worked in the open air, while the tweeded wives of the first are the only women present.

'Let's sit over there,' suggested Carolus. He had noticed that Roger was greeted with much friendliness among both sections of the community.

'O.K.,' said Roger, voicing the Americanism which Carolus detested most.

With drinks before them they seemed to hesitate on the brink of some remarkable confidence which was about to be broken, but Carolus gave no sign of eagerness to hear its nature. Roger, therefore, it seemed, did not open the conversation.

'Lot of people seem to come here on Sunday morning,' Carolus commented.

'Yes. It's always like this on Sunday mornings.'

'I see your father over there,' said Carolus.

'I saw him. But we don't Speak,' replied Roger.

'Isn't that Warton Leng, the organist?'

'Yes. Church must be finished, then.'

'You don't go?'

'No. I never seem to have taken to it, somehow. The old woman goes. You've met her, haven't you?'

'Yes, indeed,' said Carolus, remembering Estelle Delafont, *née*, and to be correct still, Flo Carver.

Then Roger approached slightly nearer to the Subject—or was it the Subject?

'You've also met June Mockett,' he said almost accusingly.

'I have. In Swindleton's office,' Carolus replied.

'I wish she wouldn't go there,' said Roger pettishly. 'You see June and I are going to be married.'

'Congratulations. But why mustn't she go to Swindleton's office? I thought she worked there.'

'She does. For the present. I want to get her to leave. I don't like the place. And I don't like Swindleton. He's a creep.'

'I see. She's a very pretty girl. You're lucky.'

'That's what that stepfather of mine—so-called—tells me. He'd better keep away from June, too.'

'You mean Mr Delafont?' asked Carolus innocently.

'Yes. Honestly, Mr Deene, he's a nasty piece of work, taking pot all day long. I could never understand what mum sees in him.'

'Is it his colour you object to?'

'No. It's not that. It's just that he ... I don't know. I can't stand him.'

'Well you'll be leaving home soon, when you get married.'

'I don't know when that'll be. Not till this business about Dutch has been cleared up, anyway.'

'Why? What has that to do with your getting married?'

Roger's face clouded.

'Some people seem to suspect me of having something to do with Dutch's death.'

'On what grounds?'

'None! But you know how beastly suspicious some

people are. They don't know who else to suspect so they suspect me.' Roger paused, then turned towards Carolus. 'Do you, Mr Deene?' he asked.

Carolus answered coolly.

'Not particularly. I suspect everyone till I have reason *not* to suspect them. What is it you wanted to tell me?'

'Oh, that. It may not have anything to do with it. And it'll look as though I'm trying to put your suspicions on someone else.'

'But you're not?'

'I've no reason to. This is all it is. June lives just across the road from the Spook Club. Swindleton owns the house she lives in and several more round there. June's house is divided up into flats. He lets one of these on the first floor to June and her mother. I tell her it's because he wants to keep an eye on her, but she won't admit it. She thinks it's just kindness. Kindness, mind you! From Swindleton. However there it is and June and I often sit up at the window after her mother's gone to bed and watch who goes in and comes out of the Spook Club. I tell you, Mr Deene, you'd be surprised. Some of the most so-called respectable people in the town going in to buy pot. My so-called stepfather among them.'

'Go on. This is interesting.'

'I'm glad you find it so,' said Roger bitterly. 'On the Saturday night on which Dutch disappeared...'

'How do you mean "disappeared"?'

'Well he was never seen again, was he? And he was found dead next night. On the Saturday night we sat up there till late. We knew there was something funny going on over at the Spook Club but of course we hadn't an idea what...'

Carolus interrupted.

'Stop a minute,' he said. 'Wasn't your friend June a hostess at the Spook Club? How did she come to be free on a Saturday evening?'

Roger grinned.

'She doesn't take her duties too seriously,' he said. 'That evening, at any rate, she didn't intend to go there. It must have been not long before midnight when Des and Phil came out together and rode away.'

'You didn't see them again that night?'

'No, but I'll tell you what we did see. Swindleton came out of the Club about an hour later.'

'That was around twelve?'

'So far as I can say. I didn't keep looking at my watch every five minutes, but near enough it must have been an hour after Des and Phil had left. It was early for him. Dancing usually went on till much later.'

'You've no idea why he packed up early?'

'No. We were surprised. I said to June, Swindleton's packing up early tonight. Anyway he came out, got in his car and went off.'

'Did he lock up?'

'Must have done. I don't remember seeing him but he locks up every night.'

'Is that all you saw?'

'No. This is the bit I want to tell you. This is what I haven't told anyone else.'

'Go on.'

'Well, it must have been about another half hour or so after Swindleton had gone that another motor-bike came up. It wasn't Phil or Des. I know their bikes well. But all the same I recognized who it was. So did June. It was Gil Bodmin.'

'Are you sure?'

'Absolutely. It was the biggest surprise of my life.

The skinheads never come round to the Spook Club.
Never been known to. It's kind of understood. They
go to the Cattle Market and we go to the Spook
Club.'

'So you class yourself as a greaser, if that's the
term?'

'I don't class myself as anything. Only that's what
Dutch was and I've never had any use for skinheads.
I don't mind admitting that even though I am telling
you this about one of them.

'Anyhow it was Gil. He pulled his bike up on the
stand and went round to the back door. We couldn't
see him for a bit then. But we kept watching. I told
you we thought there was something funny going on
over at the Club and this was the bit that surprised
us most. Then all of a sudden we saw Gil coming round
the corner as though Satan was after him. He pulled
his bike off the stand, jumped on and was away hell
for leather down the road.'

'Can you be sure of one or two things, Roger?'

'I should think so. I'm not likely to have forgotten
that night, am I?'

'First of all, you are absolutely certain that it was
Gil who rode up? I mean with goggles and helmets
most of you look the same.'

'Absolutely certain. He took his helmet off to go
round the back.'

'Then are you equally certain that it was Gil who
came back from behind the building?'

'Certain as the other. I watched him, didn't I? And
June will tell you the same.'

'And there was no one—please be quite sure about
this—there was no one on his pillion, coming or
going?'

'No one. We should have seen, wouldn't we? He

went off alone, same as he'd come.'

'And that was the last you saw of him? Or of anyone else round the Spook Club that night?'

'Yes. But after we'd gone to bed—June's going to marry me, remember—after we were in bed, I can't tell how long because I'd been asleep, June woke me up. She was sitting up in bed. "Roger, I'm sure I heard a car," she said. I was sleepy. "What's so funny about that?" I said, because it's a fairly busy road and you often hear cars all night. "I was asleep", I told her.

'But she went on about it. "It was stopped outside the Spook Club," she said, "and the engine was kept running."

'I asked her what sort of a car, I meant a lorry or a sports car or what. She gave me the sort of bloody silly answer a woman would give. "Just an ordinary car it sounded like." So I told her to shut up and let me get to sleep. I mean, it could have been anything. Could have been Swindleton coming back to see whether he'd locked up. Or anything. I didn't think any more about it that night. But afterwards, when I'd heard about Dutch, I wondered whether it had anything to do with it. Do you think it had?'

'I don't know,' said Carolus. It was the literal truth but it might have been called disingenuous for all that. Then he asked, 'Has your "so-called stepfather" as you refer to him, has he got a car?'

'No. A motor-bike to go to work with. He works in a factory on the other side of the town. Shares the expense of the bike with a workmate he picks up every morning. Why?'

'Just wondered,' said Carolus with annoying vagueness. 'I'll have a talk to Gil Bodmin this evening. Ask him what he was doing round the Spook Club that night.'

'Well, I must run along,' said Roger. 'I'm taking June out this afternoon.'

Now, with the latest information which Roger had given him Carolus began to feel that he was approaching the centre of the circle in ever decreasing twirls. Unless something totally unexpected turned up he believed he could give Grimsby enough information to make an arrest within the next day or two.

A nasty little case, he reflected. Full of cruelty and malice and scarcely a gleam of decent behaviour, let alone generosity or decent feeling to compensate for it.

He lunched at an arty restaurant which advertised its inclusion in some good food guide or other but would have made a Frenchman turn green not with envy but with nausea. At eleven o'clock that night, having spent some hours with his notes, he approached the Cattle Market on foot. There was a bell and a peep-hole in the door and his ringing brought out, framed in the peep-hole, a long anxious face ornamented with a ludicrous moustache.

'Are you a member?' the owner of it demanded in a tired but hostile voice.

'I've no wish to come in,' Carolus replied. 'I want to ask you if you would be good enough to call out one of your members named Gil Bodmin.'

The anxious face lengthened even more.

'I'll see if he's in the Club. Who shall I tell him wants to see him? He won't come out for just anybody you know. Are you the Law?'

'No. But he will come out if you tell him quietly, out of the hearing of any of his friends, that Carolus Deene wants to see him.'

'Who? What?'

'It's a perfectly simple name. Carolus is the Latin for Charles and Deene is quite a common surname.'

'It sounds a bit fancy. Gil won't like anything like that. But I'll try him. You wait here.'

A scowling Gil presently emerged.

'What the hell do you want?' he shouted at Carolus in the hearing of the other, then said quietly—'Wait for me round the corner.'

Carolus could hear him telling the other not to let any more of that sort in.

But presently Gil appeared and offered his hand to Carolus.

'Wasn't expecting you,' he said.

'Sure of that? What were you doing round the Spook Club on the night Dutch was killed?'

'I was going to tell you about that.'

'Then why didn't you?'

'See, it's about this phone call I got that night.'

'You didn't tell me about that, either.'

'Wait till you hear it all. It was a trap, I'm sure of that. I didn't want to get Life for killing Dutch.'

'Naturally not. Suppose you begin at the beginning?'

'Well, that Saturday was just ordinary. I was dancing at this joint, the Cattle Market, when suddenly that drip on the door you've just seen, Crumbs they call him, I don't know why, came up and told me I was wanted on the phone. A woman's voice, he said.

'I went over, just as I came when you called for me tonight and when I picked up the phone I heard this woman . . .'

'Which woman?'

'That's what I've been puzzling my brains to decide. I know I've heard the voice before but I can't make out who it was.'

'You're not the only one,' remarked Carolus.

'Anyway she said "Is that Gil Bodmin?" I said "Yes. Who are you?" She said "Never mind," but added that it was something I should be glad to hear. Then she said young Dutch Carver wanted to see me. Now you must understand with our crowd if anyone says he wants to see anyone and names a place and time it means trouble and plenty of it. Then this woman who I don't know who it was says "He's waiting down in the cellar of the Spook Club now. The door's open," and hung the receiver up. There was only one thing to do. I knew I could handle Dutch and wasn't worried about any other greasers he might have with him. So I didn't call the boys but got on my bike and went straight round to the Spook Club.

'I put my bike up on its stand and went round to the back. Sure enough as the woman had said the back door was open and what I took to be the cellar door was open, too. What's more the light was switched on.

'I went on down expecting to get a crack over the head at any minute but when I got to the bottom of the stairs I saw Dutch, strung up like a chicken and stark bollock naked. His hair had been cut short and the poor little sod was shivering with cold. He'd been gone over pretty bad and a cut in his face was bleeding. When he saw me he was more scared still and tried to turn his head away as though I shouldn't recognize him.'

'What did you do?'

'Hopped it and ——ing quick.'

'You didn't think of releasing him?'

'Yes I thought of it. But I thought too that that was just what I was meant to do. The telephone and all was a trap. The only thing was to get out of there pretty dam' quick.'

'And leave him in that state?'

'What else could I do? If I'd told the police they'd

have thought it was me. Besides, how was I to know he was going to die? He was alive enough when I was there.'

'Not very heroic of you, was it?' suggested Carolus. 'But there's been a lot of non-heroism all through this case. Even if you had told me, instead of leaving me to find out that you'd been there, I should not have thought so badly of you. As it is I shan't lift a finger to help you. Even if all you've told me is true and the Law gets on to your part in the whole thing it'll be a lagging at least, so think that over.'

Probably no one had spoken to Gil like that for years and he did not seem to be able to find an answer.

Chapter Fourteen

More for some way of filling time before he met Grimsby next evening at seven, than with any very lively hope of further discovery, Carolus decided to call on Bert Carver and Mrs Farnham at about the same time as he had been to the house before.

This time it was Bert who opened the door.

'We're going out in a few minutes,' he warned Carolus. 'But you can come in if it's anything urgent.'

'I think this whole enquiry's urgent, but you don't seem to agree,' said Carolus.

'Oh, I don't know. Of course I want to know who killed the poor little sod, only you can't expect *her* to be that interested. After all he wasn't her kid.'

'No. I see that.'

'And his own mother never had a bit of time for him. Nor for me, for the matter of that. She had too much to do looking in the mirror, she had.'

'I've met your older son,' said Carolus.

'Oh yes. Good steady boy, he is. Hard worker. Not like the other one. Mrs Farnham will be down in a minute. She's just getting ready. Was there anything particular you wanted to know?'

'Yes. Did Dutch—I seem to have got in the way of calling Kenneth that—did he confide in you at all, Mr Carver?'

'How d'you mean?'

'I know you didn't get on very well together, but after all you were his father and he lived in the same house.'

'I see what you're getting at. I can't say he did, to speak the honest truth. Not since I took up with Connie. At one time we used to have a word sometimes. Nothing much—only about dog-racing and television and that. But not for a long time now, we haven't. See where it was, he had his own friends, Des and Phil and those. As I told you before, I never saw much of him.'

'He didn't, for instance, tell you something he wanted kept secret during the last week or two?'

'What was that?'

'I don't know. I wish I did. But I know he had some secret he didn't seem able to tell anyone.'

'Perhaps it was where he got his money, though there wasn't much secret about that. He got it pushing pot for Swindleton.'

'You know that?'

'Where else could it have been? You know what Swindleton is.'

Mrs Farnham appeared.

'What's this about Swindleton?' she asked. 'I know one thing, he's not long out of prison and it won't be long before he's back again.'

'Who says so?' asked Bert. 'You've no right to say things like that. You don't know there's any truth in it. You could be taken up for putting about such stories.'

'I know all about it...'

'Yes. You always know all about it till one day you find yourself in Court. You haven't said good evening to Mr Deene, either.'

Connie Farnham's 'good evening' was dropped snappily and she turned to Bert.

'Come on,' she said. 'We've got to hurry.'

Carolus left them and made for the Spook Club. It wasn't open yet but he found Swindleton in his office. The man appeared to Carolus even more nervous than before. He was smoking a cigarette and a piled ash-tray gave evidence that he had been doing so for some time.

'Yes? Yes?' he said rising to his feet.

'I have a few more questions for you, Swindleton.'

'Oh God! Shan't I ever hear the last of this wretched business. What is it about this time?'

'About the Saturday night on which Dutch Carver was killed in your cellar.'

'Who says he was? It may have been anywhere.'

'You said you closed the Club early that night because the woman's voice on the phone told you to?'

Swindleton looked at Carolus as though wondering if he should deny it.

'I was tired,' he said. 'Don't you think a man gets tired at my job? I get so tired sometimes I could drop.'

'Were Phil and Des tired when they left the club about an hour before you?'

'I don't know. I never saw them go. Well not actually leave.'

'Where did you go when you left your Club?'

'Home, of course. Where do you think? I went home to get some sleep.'

'And did you sleep well, Swindleton? Knowing all you did?'

'Knowing what? I knew nothing. I slept like a top. Nothing on *my* conscience. You make things up, Mr Deene!'

'You didn't come back that night?'

'To the Spook Club? Certainly not. I didn't wake up till the morning.'

'You've no idea who might have gone back there?'

'None at all. I only know that when I got there in the morning Dutch had been taken away.'

'I'm going to have a look round that cellar,' announced Carolus.

'You can, Mr Deene. You won't find much. The police have been all over it, every inch of it. But you can look. Certainly you can.'

Carolus went down to the cellar and from the top of the stairs Swindleton watched him. He saw Carolus peer about him, using his torch, then stoop down and pick something from the floor. This he put between the pages of a pocket diary and prepared to join Swindleton.

'What have you got?' asked the *discothècaire* anxiously.

Carolus replied in one word.

'Evidence,' he said.

Swindleton looked apoplectic but ignoring his supplications to inform him, Carolus went out to his car. From behind him on the kerb Carolus heard Swindleton's protestations of innocence, of ignorance, of the best intentions as he drove away.

He reached the Wheatsheaf in time for his appointment and found Grimsby waiting for him. The two talked for a long time over their drinks in a quiet corner of the bar. Finally Carolus seemed to be summing it up when he said—'What it looks like is that it all depends on whether a little girl of twelve keeps her word to a young blackguard or not. And if she does we may never clear up this case.'

'Something like that. Of course, she may have forgotten by now. Little girls of that age have short memories.'

'No,' said Carolus. 'I don't think Liz will have forgotten. Which reminds me—I want to show you something.'

Carolus took out his pocket diary and from its interior produced a strand of hair, about four inches long.

'What's this?' asked Grimsby.

'One for the forensic experts. I'm sure you found some hair in Swindleton's cellar which had escaped being burnt. What I want to know is if this matches up and—if they can say—was it cut off at about the same time.'

Grimsby smiled.

'So you have to come to us for that sort of thing? It's all very well, Carolus, but you expect what you call the forensic experts to do all the work, then you weigh in with a spectacular solution which may or may not be the correct one.'

'I know! Shameful, isn't it? But you have all the facilities and I'm just an amateur. Hullo, what's the matter with Goad?'

'I didn't know he was here,' said Grimsby.

'He had just been called out to the phone and he's coming over here in a hurry.'

Goad was in civvies, but though he moved quickly as Carolus had said there seemed to be nothing excited about his haste.

'There's a pretty violent fight on in the Spook Club,' he said quite calmly, 'between skinheads and greasers, I gather. If you think it's any concern of yours come on down and see it.'

Carolus and Grimsby drank up and followed Inspector Goad to the door.

'We'll take my car,' said Grimsby. 'I shouldn't like to see your beautiful paintwork damaged.'

They did this and Carolus wondered as they drew up whether behind the blinds of the house opposite Roger and June were watching.

The strangest thing they noticed as they went down to the cellar was the absence of noise. There must have been a dozen youths mawling, kicking, landing powerful blows on one another and yet beyond a few grunts and the sound of scuffling there was almost no sound.

Carolus saw Gil Bodmin at once. His shirt was torn to rags and his big fists flayed about, not aimlessly but with purposeful effect. He heard an ugly sound as Gil landed a powerful blow on—Phil was it? The long-haired boy went down to the floor and tried to protect his head from the boots that milled around and over him. Gil at once looked for other prey and seeing a youngster among the greasers lifted him bodily and threw him into the most crowded collection of the enemy.

Two of these had bottles which had been broken off against the wall. They held these by the necks with their rings of jagged glass pointing outward, and with their backs to the wall waited the onslaught of Gil and his friends. It was apparent that the offensive was taken by the skinheads while the greasers who were fewer in number held a defensive though no less aggressive role.

From among the skinhead ranks Trimmer suddenly broke loose and Carolus saw that he held a knife, a dangerous-looking thing such as those with which the Commandos had been armed during the war. He was about to take it away from Trimmer, who appeared to be insane, when the police came down the cellar steps and went to work on the combatants.

There were at least fourteen of them and they spread out across the cellar and advanced shoulder to shoulder like the Greeks or Romans in ancient battles. Within three minutes of their entrance order was restored and there was time to examine the damage among the boys who had fought. There was quite a lot of blood about and one boy had received a knife wound in the shoulder, another was moaning and holding his head which had been knocked back violently against the wall.

A big sergeant demanded—'What was it all about?'

'Skinheads!' said Des Grayne and made as if to spit.

'Greasers!' responded Trimmer, but Gil Bodmin said nothing.

The Sergeant addressed himself to him, Gil, specifically.

'What were you doing down here? This isn't your manor.'

Gil said sulkily—'We were bored. We came visiting.'

'Oh you did, did you? You'll come and visit the Station, Bodmin. We've had enough trouble with you. Who let you in here?'

'Who do you think? The hero of the greasers, Mister Swindleton.'

Swindleton who had remained near the top of the steps said—'That's not true, Sergeant. I never let them in here. I don't want them round my place. They always cause trouble.'

'Oh, shut your mouth,' said Gil. 'You know you telephoned for us and said the cellar door was open.'

'I didn't!' cried Swindleton hysterically. 'I never did anything of the sort! They came on their own without any sort of warning and rushed down to the cellar. My boys were quite unprepared.'

'Your boys?' said Des. 'Who are you calling your

boys? Just because some of us used your lousy Club. If you mean those that push pot for you...'

Swindleton became dignified. 'Des!' he said in an injured voice. 'I'm surprised at you!'

But no one else was, it seemed, and the police started taking the boys upstairs one after another to the waiting van.

'Don't start trouble now,' said the Sergeant, looking at Gil. 'It won't do you any good.'

After a moment Gil seemed to agree and went with the rest though with an ugly expression of defiance on his face.

Carolus was surprised to see, in a very poor condition and being helped towards the stairs Roger Carver. As he passed Carolus he said sarcastically, 'Thank you *very* much. Nice way of keeping a confidence, I must say.'

'There was no confidence,' Carolus replied.

'Not for you, evidently,' said Roger with heightened sarcasm. 'I suppose what I told you was meant to be shouted round to all the skinheads in town, wasn't it?'

'There was no obligation on me to hush up anything you told me. You seemed pleased enough to talk yourself,' said Carolus. 'But if you want to know your name was never mentioned to Gil Bodmin by me.'

'Then what brought the skinheads down here?' asked Roger. 'They were looking for me.'

Carolus said nothing more but did not feel very pleased with himself. It was true that Gil Bodmin must have gathered how Carolus had obtained his information about Gil's late visit that Saturday night to the Spook Club and it might be that he had acted on it and caused the barney Carolus had just witnessed. On the other hand it could have been as Gil said, that Swindleton had telephoned to the skinheads that their enemy were trapped in the cellar and the door was open.

'What was all that about?' asked Grimsby when the police had taken Roger away.

'You'll hear it all later,' promised Carolus. 'He accused me of breaking faith with him.'

'And had you?'

'I suppose I may have done in a way. At least I'm not quite happy about it.'

'What now?' asked Grimsby.

'Goad's over there. Ask him whether he would like to hear what little bits I've managed to string together. If so we'll go up to his place or better still, ask him if he will come over to Newminster.'

'I'll try. He reads whodunnits so he might like to hear what you've got to say.'

'Bad logic, but it might work. I've got one last job to do then I'll be with you.'

Grimsby nodded and hurried in pursuit of the Inspector. Carolus drove to 47 Docker Street.

He found Liz indoors—evidently Mrs Bodmin was taking her guardianship seriously. But Liz was alone and when Carolus came in from the street she announced quite gleefully.

'I'm not allowed out.'

'Who said so?'

'Mum did. She says the coalman will take me away in a sack if I go out alone.'

That surely was stretching it a little far, thought Carolus, but nodded gravely.

'Where is your mum?' he asked.

'She's in the lavortree,' said Liz.

That produced a silence between them which lasted until Mrs Bodmin appeared.

'Now Liz,' she said, 'you be a good girl and go and

play with Freda Nustle for a little while. I'll call for you when I've finished talking to this gentleman.'

'Don't want to,' said Liz.

'Now run along and don't be naughty, otherwise you know what it'll be.'

'Freda Nustle says coalmen don't put little girls in sacks.'

'You tell her she's a story then, because your mum says they do, if you don't behave yourself. Now run along with you!'

As soon as the child had gone out Mrs Bodmin nodded vigorously to Carolus.

'I've got it all out of her. Every word. Only I've written it down because I couldn't bear to talk about it. It's wicked, that's what it is and if there's a God in heaven he'll know the punishment. I'm sure I can't think of one bad enough.'

Out of the drawer in the dresser she brought out some sheets of paper and handed them to Carolus.

'Now you mind what you do with that,' she said. 'Because I don't want my little girl's name talked about, nor me either for not looking after her, though how I could be expected to when I'm at work all day I *don't* know, and her only twelve. It's a pity her father isn't alive because he'd have something to say, you can be sure of that. What makes it worse is that Liz is a good little girl and not a bit like that, or anything of the sort. It makes you feel queer to think about it, and to think it was going on all that time and me having no idea about it. I don't know!

'Anyway you tell anyone you have to tell, otherwise keep it to yourself. As I say it's not something you want talked about, is it?'

'What about Liz? Do you think she'll talk about it. To her friend Freda, for example?'

'She'd be ashamed. I feel certain of that. Look at the
way she wouldn't tell me for a long time and then
came out with it all of a sudden. She's a funny child
but I don't think she'd ever talk to Freda Nustle, *or*
anyone else. 'Ark at them now, the way they're enjoy-
ing themselves! That's Mrs Donkin's little boy they're
running after. They'll have his big sister after them
in a minute and she'll give them what for. That's
children for you—they must be making a noise or
getting up to mischief. Not that Liz is as bad as some,
or Freda either. Only where it is, her mother likes a
drop now and again and it's not good for her with
that indigestion she's got. I mean she's all wind and the
last thing she should take is light ale. If I ever take
anything, which is seldom, I like a drop of gin. That
does you good, I always say, not these gassy drinks.
But I suppose you have to keep off it on your job. It
would never do for you to get muddled between one
and another when you're trying to find out the truth
about anything, would it?'

Carolus was determined not to break the flow which
he enjoyed. But Mrs Bodmin herself seemed to do so.

'Well, I must See About something,' she said. 'This'll
never do. And you keep what's on that paper to yourself, except what you have to tell the police. You'll
find it all there. Every word of it. And I only wish I
didn't have to write it, but sometimes you can't keep
things to yourself, can you?'

Carolus did not feel that an answer was necessary.

Chapter Fifteen

'I'm having a few friends in this evening,' said Carolus to Mrs Stick next day. 'Perhaps we could have a cold buffet?'

'Buffets, sir, I thought those were the places on railway stations where you get sandwiches.'

Carolus smiled.

'We shall have sandwiches too, Mrs Stick. Only better ones I hope. You see I want you and Stick to come as guests.'

'As guests, sir? Then who's going to get everything ready, I'd like to know? Besides, it wouldn't be Right.'

'Mr Gorringer is coming,' said Carolus encouragingly.

'I shouldn't mind that so much, not after we went on that cruise with him. Only, what I say is...'

'You come, Mrs Stick, because tonight will be the last word on the case which you and Stick started me off on.'

'You mean about that poor young boy that was killed falling off his motor-bike?'

'You can put it like that. At least you know what I'm talking about.'

'I daresay Stick will, he having a good memory for

anything like that. He told me at the time he'd never forget accidentally getting hold of one of the boy's hands and finding it like an icicle.'

Mr Gorringer was no more enthusiastic about the occasion in prospect.

'While I appreciate your including myself in your audience, my dear Deene, I cannot but feel that on this occasion I have played a very minor role in your investigations. It scarcely merits the privilege you offer me.'

'I might say that all you did on this occasion was to remind me of when term would start. But I shan't do that, if only for the sake of your interest in other cases, I do hope you will care to hear the few details I have to give.'

'Most assuredly,' said Mr Gorringer. 'Most assuredly. You will, I surmise, invite Hollingbourne since he was able to furnish you with certain details of the victim's conduct?'

'Hollingbourne has taken his brood to a holiday camp, I understand. Won't be back till a day or two before term begins.'

'Ah yes. Very appropriate,' said the Headmaster ambiguously.

So it was to a small very mixed audience of Inspector Goad, Detective Sergeant Grimsby, the Sticks and Mr Gorringer that Carolus gave his recital of the case which he now considered completed.

'As soon as I went out to examine the body which Stick had found I was convinced that things were not what they seemed. It was all too perfect a discovery to be true. You know how it is with evidence—you accept it or you feel there's something planted there. There were here the marks on wrists and ankles to show how the boy had been taken to that point in the road on a motor-bicycle, the shorn hair, the naked-ness—these things told me very clearly what I was *meant* to think. I, or whoever else came on the body would obligingly say "Yes. A young greaser with his hair cut short. A member of some town gang who has fallen out with the rest of them. A boy who has been deliberately humiliated and then murdered. To dis-pose of the body some motor-cyclist among them has tied his feet to the footrests and his arms about the rider's waist and taken him across country to the place pre-arranged to dump his body. The police will im-mediately search for a young tearabout who owes the boy a grudge." This was all so obvious that it made me turn in exactly the opposite direction, though I noted that Grimsby at first accepted the thing. "Been carried some distance on the pillion seat of a motor-bike," he told me flatly.'

'That was in the first days,' Grimsby reminded Carolus. But Carolus began speculating.

'Suppose,' he said, 'that someone quite other than a hippy or anything of the sort, wanted to get young Carver out of the way, how would he go about it in a manner that would throw suspicion on someone else? Exactly as he did, I decided. The boy was already known to associate with a pretty poor crowd of villains in the making. What more probable than that he had fallen out with one group or the other? To be safe the murderer decided that both the skinheads *and* the greasers who had been Carver's friends should be involved in his death and set about this by black-mailing the wretched owner of the discotheque fre-quented by Carver to bribe Phil White and Des Grayne to beat up Dutch, cut his hair and leave him in the cellar of the Spook Club tied up, naked, for someone else to kill. Not satisfied with this, before actually taking Dutch's life, he arranged to bring Gil Bodmin to the scene in the hope that he would add his evidence of murder, Gil being regarded as the leader of the local gang of skinheads.

'So we come to the mysterious woman's voice on the telephone. She it was who told Swindleton he was to get Phil and Des down to his cellar, she it was who rang Gil Bodmin at the Cattle Market, the meeting-place of the skinheads, and persuaded him to go to the cellar of the Spook Club after Dutch had been what was expressively known as "done up". Of this voice each hearer said that he *thought* he had heard it somewhere and so on, but no one could identify it. We shall come to that again.

'To go back to the suppositions that started the case for me. They were chiefly negative. I did *not* think that Dutch had been murdered by the teenage monsters of Hartington, though several of them seemed quite capable of murder. This for a time and purely by supposition put out of reckoning as suspects Phil, Des, Gil Bodmin and the most unpleasant of them all known as Trimmer. After that it became a question of motive. Who on earth among adults could want Dutch so much out of the way that he was prepared to adopt the difficult and dangerous scheme to kill the boy and put the potential blame on someone else? Who, and with what motive?'

There was a rumbling sound in the room caused by Mr Gorringer clearing his throat as he was accustomed to do when he wished to attract attention.

'I perceive, my dear Deene, that you are about to name the villain of the piece. Let us therefore pause for a moment to prolong the period of our curiosity.'

'By all means. Have a drink,' said Carolus.

Mrs Stick spoke up.

'Upon my word it doesn't bear thinking about,' she said. 'To think that's what you've been finding out about all this time! If I'd known what Stick had come on I'd have told him to leave it be.'

'But I haven't got nearly so far as Mr Gorringer supposes,' Carolus said. 'We are asking as yet no more than Who? and with what motive? To answer those questions took a considerable time and much expert work by Detective Sergeant Grimsby. I did not even at once see that the obvious answer to the second question was the ugly word Blackmail. Dutch Carver was blackmailing someone and doing fairly well out of it. For although I quite believed that he was a pusher for Swindleton, disposing of odd quantities of cannabis, I did not think that Swindleton's resources enabled him to put up any real sum in capital. He was blackmailing someone else, and I know one cruel truth about that. The blackmailee in this or in any other crime does not need to be rich. The poor wretch who is being held to ransom will find *some* means *somehow* to satisfy the blackmailer who has sufficient hold over him. It is the appalling part of this trade. A man will beg, borrow or even commit crimes to try the impossible task of buying off the greedy blackguard who holds him. So I did not necessarily suppose that I must look for a rich man as the murderer of Dutch. There were a number of possibilities.

'When I began to think it might be somehow concerned with the little girl, Liz Bodmin, it narrowed it down somewhat but it was all very hypothetical. And Liz would not, or perhaps could not talk. There was pathos in the child keeping silence in loyalty to the young ruffian whom she thought to be alive, keeping a silence the breaking of which, had she known it, would have revealed the identity of his murderer. I felt bound for a time to respect that silence and approach the matter from another angle.

'*If*, and you will note that we are still confined by the ifs, if Dutch was levelling blackmail, as I thought, on what grounds? Who was guilty of what? Before the legislation popularly known as the Abse Act had been passed there would not have been much doubt of it for Dutch was younger than what is so insanely called the age of consent, and so could both share the offence and levy blackmail from the other partner. But even a British jury with all their narrow-mindedness and prejudices would hesitate to send a man to prison for an act with such a hardened young rapscallion as Dutch Carver. If not queerness, therefore, what? The answer was close at hand. Someone had corrupted the child whose arrested development and freedom from maternal supervision made her singularly vulnerable, and Dutch had discovered it and bound Liz to him with the strongest bonds of secrecy.

'So finally I came to the final "Who", the one that could only be revealed by Liz herself. There were several possibilities if we remember the Moors murders, and how a woman was involved in those. I did not for some reason—perhaps a failure in my knowledge of sexual psychology—suspect a woman acting alone, but there were two women, both capable of vicious practices I believed, and both with a man who might be capable of sharing them, Connie Farnham and Flo Carver (or Estelle Delafont as she liked to call herself). The second one had a man friend, the coloured Justus Delafont who in spite of their protestations of freedom from colour prejudice, many English people would suspect. But what possible evidence was there to connect them with this filthy crime?'

'A well-merited condemnation,' put in Mr Gorringer.
'I do not remember an investigation of yours, my dear
Deene, which has brought you so near to the devil and
all his works.'

'Shocking!' said Mrs Stick and her husband nodded
agreement with her.

'Revolting,' said Grimsby.

But Goad, who knew more of the unpleasant mani-
festations of vice than any of them merely nodded in
invitation to Carolus to continue.

'I decided,' he said, 'to steal Skilly's motorcar.' This
caused a certain disturbance in the room but Carolus
remained calm.

'I doubt if I heard you aright,' boomed Mr Gorringer. 'To steal a motorcar?'

'Only temporarily,' said Carolus, 'it was returned to
the owner the next day.'

'After you had gone over the boot with a fine tooth-
comb,' suggested Grimsby.

'Exactly. As you had done with the cellar. You must
forgive me for a small deception between profession-
als. I gave you the blond hair I found in the boot
from my pocket-case, whereas I had found another hair
in the cellar which I put between the pages of my
diary. Both were specimens of the hair cut from Dutch
but the one from the boot of Skilly's car showed that
Dutch's body *after* his hair had been cut, had been
shoved into the boot of the car, and presumably,
driven across to the Boxley Road. This is what I suspected. The marks on wrists and ankles had been made
quite deliberately to mislead whoever would find him.
Besides I had thought when I first looked at the body
that its hunched-up position, stiffened by *rigor mortis*,
could be due either to the boy being tied on to a
pillion and carried by the motor-cyclist, or could have

been thrust into the boot of a car. I felt the latter was more probable for reasons I have given.

'This was a good leap forward. I knew the murderer was one or two of three persons, or conceivably all the three. The choirmaster Leng, his friend and cousin-in-law Skilly, or perhaps in a minor role helping to cover up for her husband, Leng's wife. What I needed to know was who had corrupted Liz, who had paid out blackmail to Dutch, and who had murdered him and attempted to put the blame on the teenagers. This person, I was convinced, was one and the same, though I have not discovered yet which of the other two had assisted him, if either. The voice on the telephone could be either that of Mrs Leng, or of Skilly who by the look of him might be able to give a fairly useful imitation of a woman's voice. That, if he has not already done so, will be for Detective Sergeant Grimsby to discover. But the triumph is Mrs Bodmin's. She it was who without apparently dampening the high spirits of her little daughter Liz, obtained from her the information that we all need. Inspector Goad and Detective Sergeant Grimsby are welcome to examine the curious and not I'm afraid quite literate script but from it they will discover quite certainly that the man who was being blackmailed and murdered his blackmailer, who pushed his naked corpse with hair duly cut to give the impression that other young men had been at work, was the supposed beneficiary of the dead boy, Warton Leng.

'When you two policemen with your expertise which you have also made available to me, have tidied up the odd ends, I don't see very much prospect of freedom for Leng for the next twenty or thirty years, though doubtless he will be able to play the church organ on Sundays.'

'A most dastardly affair, and I for one am delighted that you have brought the perpetrator to justice,' Mr Gorringer exulted.

'What strikes me is the stupidity of Leng,' said Goad. 'Did he really think that any competent CID officer was going to be fooled by his wrist marks and ankle marks and cropped hair?'

'It damned nearly fooled me,' said Grimsby frankly. 'With all the motor-bikes in the case I doubt if I should have suspected a car being used. And then what June called "just an ordinary car", in other words not Leng's but Skilly's little Cortina. How wrong Roger was to think perhaps the best piece of evidence we had was the sort of bloody silly answer a woman would give.'

'I should think so!' said Mrs Stick. 'To my mind it's the women who should have all the credit in this case. Mrs Bodmin for finding out from her little girl who was to blame, June for noticing that car that drew up at the Spook Club to take the poor young boy away, and...'

'Mrs Stick for persuading her husband to tell me of the corpse he had found. Yes, I quite agree, Mrs Stick. Only if we search farther back was not the boy's mother in part to blame?'

'Because she never bothered to bring the boy up, you mean?' asked Mrs Stick nodding. 'I'm sure we all agree with you there. We read in the paper every day of parents not caring about their children and here's a case of it, if ever there was one!'

'What about Mrs Bodmin?' asked Stick joining in the discussion for the first time.

'Well, she did learn better, didn't she, in the end? Let's hope the little girl will be brought up properly after this and not let run about on the streets after all we're told on the telly about nasty old men with bags of sweets to tempt them. I know if I had a little daughter ...'

'Which you haven't,' said Stick somewhat obviously.

But Carolus himself was to have a nasty surprise before he could feel that the case was quite completed.

'Tell me,' he asked Grimsby. 'When are you going to arrest Leng?'

'Oh come now Carolus. Don't be naïve. Leng was charged with murder twenty-four hours ago.'

'Really? On what evidence?'

'Pretty much what you have given,' said Grimsby. 'You've been enormously helpful, Carolus, but don't take the police for complete fools.'

'Far from it, I assure you,' said Carolus.

'It is an excellent example of what I am always telling you, Deene. Let the cobbler stick to his last. Your duty is with Upper Fifth's historical studies.'

'Then perhaps we shouldn't have so many murders about the house,' said Mrs Stick.

'Or so many whodunnits,' said Inspector Goad, 'and that to my mind would be a pity. Good night, ladies and gentlemen. And I may appropriately bid you to sleep well.'